For Cleo, m... good friend

Always,
Phyllis

YOU NEVER KNOW

PHYLLIS KIEFFE

Sometimes the road to love can get a little bit bumpy

CHAPTER 1

The Vincent Thomas Bridge span is so long that it connects the City of Long Beach, one of California's largest cities and busiest harbors, to San Pedro, the site of the Port of Los Angeles, the nation's busiest port. As you drive across the bridge, you can't help but marvel at all the bustling activities of the two harbors beneath you. The 200-foot-tall container cranes stretch endlessly into the sky. You can even see cruise ships departing, continuously, from the World Cruise Center in the Los Angeles Port and the Queen Mary, which is now a full-service hotel, docked in the Long Beach harbor. The Aquarium of the Pacific is located next to one of the main Catalina Express terminals and is, also, in the Long Beach Harbor.

San Pedro is a unique slice of the Port of Los Angeles. It is in the process of renovating the Ports O' Call, a longtime waterfront attraction. It will be renamed the San Pedro Public Market. Many say it will be San Pedro's version of San Francisco's Fisherman's Wharf. San Pedro is often compared to San Francisco with its hilly streets and ocean views. There are many memorable sites in the San Pedro Harbor area, such as the Merchant Marine Memorial and the Los Angeles Maritime Museum. And

1

also, the huge Korean Friendship Bell which is located a little further inland.

San Pedro is a very colorful and diverse cultural community which makes it so charming. It is known for its outstanding ethnic restaurants. Most of them are owner owned and serve delicious dishes unique to their origin. As you walk by their restaurants the wonderful aromas permeate the air.

Rising behind San Pedro is the prestigious city of Palos Verdes. Palos Verdes is noted for its exclusive residential areas and equestrian estates, all in the seven to eight-dollar figure range. This is the area where Donna Taylor lived. Donna loved driving across the Vincent Thomas Bridge to her beautiful townhome in Palos Verdes. She loved the smell of the ocean air and the feel of the wind blowing through her hair. She felt the bridge was the connection to her home and the family she loved, and it was.

CHAPTER 2

It's been said that some people are born with a silver spoon in their mouth. That was definitely Donna. She had everything and more. She was single, in her early thirties, very pretty with long, blonde, thick hair and bright blue eyes. Her classes in Yoga and Pilates helped to keep her mind sharp and her petite 5'4" body shapely. Donna was an only child and came from a very wealthy family. Her mother had passed away a few years ago, but she was a major influence in Donna's upbringing. Her mother always instilled in her how important it was to give back. That was probably why she donated almost all of her time to charity work and raising money to help those in need. Her father, Don, had faithfully helped her to continue with this commitment. Donna's father and his boxer dog, Murphy, were the center of her family now. She would always miss her mother, but she was definitely a Daddy's Girl, and she was named after her father, Don. Her father had made his fortune in real estate specializing in apartment buildings, and made sure Donna had everything she needed or wanted. He had purchased an expensive townhouse for her recently which she loved. It was located just as you started to drive into the exclusive area of Palos Verdes, and was not far from her father's estate in the same area. Donna usually stopped by her father's place on her way home from work just to visit with him and play with his loveable boxer, Murphy. He was a great "sounding board" and had big shoulders to lean on. She always listened to his advice because he was usually right and she followed it. Her father and Murphy were definitely the light of her life. Donna loved her life. She worked tirelessly for various charities and did fundraising for many organizations in the community.

Donna dated off and on but did not meet anyone that met her expectations. She was independent and liked being by herself. She felt free to take off on short trips, especially, to Catalina several times a year. San Pedro had its own Catalina Express terminal which was very convenient for her. She loved the residents in Catalina and knew many of the shopkeepers. Her townhouse was filled with beautiful treasures made from the local artisans and craftsmen there, as well as natives in other countries.

When she had guests, they always commented on her beautiful treasures and asked if she was a world traveler. She didn't have the heart to tell them she was just a local traveler. Men always told her that her place was exotic. She loved that. That was her favorite compliment.

When Donna needed to get away, she could hardly wait to jump on the Catalina Express boat in the San Pedro Harbor and be on the island in 45 minutes. About 20 minutes from Catalina's shore, dolphins might appear gliding in unison next to the boat, gracefully leaping in and out of the water. Donna said it was like they were accompanying everyone on the boat to the island.

CHAPTER 3

David was in his late thirties. Single, very good looking, 6'4", about 210-220lbs, thick dark hair and physically fit. He jogged about 5 miles every morning and went to the gym on a regular basis. He took good care of himself and did not smoke or drink excessively. He was conservative and lived in an apartment in San Pedro. He came from a well-to-do family in the Palos Verdes area.

His father, John Collins, was widowed. He acquired his wealth from real estate, mainly in apartment buildings, and he wanted the same for his son.

When David finished college, his dad took him aside and said, "Let's see what you can do, David."

His father transferred ownership of one his apartment buildings, which was not doing well, to David.

"Thank you, Dad, that's very generous."

The apartments needed renovating badly, both inside and out, and the rents were below market value with quite a few vacancies.

David was very ambitious and immediately started to work. He hired capable workmen to help him. They renovated the apartments inside and out and added a fresh coat of paint both inside and out. When he was finished, the building didn't look like the same building. David put out a vacancy sign right away. He increased the rents to market value and also raised the rent, appropriately, for the existing tenants. In no time at all the apartments were filled and showing a healthy and much improved income. The transformation was amazing.

His father said "I'm impressed, son, I hope the tenants don't get confused about where they live. Let's go to dinner to celebrate!"

They went to a fine restaurant and no expense was spared. It was the kind of restaurant noted for its superb food and outstanding wines. The booths were far enough apart, which allowed for private conversation, and the waiter actually placed a napkin across your lap.

Over drinks his father asked, "What are your plans now, David?"

"You mean for this property, Dad?"

"Yes."

"Well, I would like to turn it and buy another when the market looks better. It's a great time to buy now but, unfortunately not to sell."

"I like your thinking son. David, I'd like you to scout around and find another apartment that you think would be a good investment. Then I'd like to give you a few bucks to help you buy it. What do you think?"

"That would be very generous, again, of you, Dad."

They toasted their drinks and ordered dinner.

It wasn't long before David spotted another apartment in trouble. He showed it to his father and said

"What do you think, Dad?"

"Go for it, son."

David made the same renovations to this building as he had done to the last. The market started to turn up and David started making a significant profit. His portfolio was rising and so was his bank account. David loved to work hard, but he also liked to play hard. He had an eye and weakness for beautiful women, and they for him. He was not only unusually handsome and charismatic, but a charmer as well.

CHAPTER 4

Donna's phone rang.

> "Hi Donna, this is Sheila, Bob and I are having a little cocktail party this Saturday night, drinks and appetizers, around 6:30. Can you come?"

Sheila and Bob Peters were Donna's best friends and lived close to her in Palos Verdes. Donna knew what this was about. This was a setup. They usually had someone they wanted her to meet.

> "Sure Sheila, what can I bring?"

> "Just yourself. See you then. Bye-bye."

Donna had met Sheila and Bob at USC, the University of Southern California. They had been classmates and have been the best of friends ever since. They had been happily married for eight years; no children, but had a very large Rottweiler dog named Buster.

Donna brought an appetizer to Sheila and Bob's party. She saw that she knew most of the people there and had worked with them on several benefits and events. Donna was waiting for the "set up". She saw Sheila heading towards her. Here it comes she thought. It looked like she was leading someone behind her. When they were closer she thought, Bingo! I hope he's for me. He was very good looking, about 6'3" or 4, well-built with thick black hair.

"Donna, I'd like you to meet David Collins. David, Donna Taylor."

David was equally impressed with Donna.

"Can I get you a drink, Donna?"

"That sounds great."

"What would you like?"

"A white wine sounds good."

"I'll bring appetizers for us, too."

When he returned, he said "I've known Sheila and Bob for a long time. They think very highly of you."

Donna replied, "And I feel the same about them. What do you do David?"

"I invest in real estate, primarily apartment buildings."

"Oh, that's what my father did before he retired."

"I'd really love to talk to him sometime."

"He would love that David. I'll warn you ahead of time, he will never stop talking about investing in apartments."

"Donna, I am so glad I met you tonight but unfortunately, I'm going to have to leave a little early."

"I wish I could have rescheduled this business meeting. Could I have your phone number?"

"Of course." Donna gave it to him.

"Thank you, Donna, I hope to see you soon."

Sheila and Bob came running over after he left.

"What did you think Donna?"

"I'm very impressed."

"Are you going to see him again?"

"He has my number."

"Oh, I hope so. We thought you and David might hit it off. You are both such free spirits. We knew he couldn't stay long tonight, he's always so busy at work. But we thought it was worth a try and it just might work out."

Donna laughed, "Well we will see."

CHAPTER 5

David called Donna the following week.

"Hi, Donna, I hope you remember me, David Collins?"

"Of course, I do." She, thought, how could I forget?

"I was calling you to see if you would like to go to dinner this Saturday?"

"Yes, that sounds good," and gave him her address.

"I'll come by around 7:00."

"See you then. Bye"

At 7:00 sharp, Donna heard the rev of an engine which sounded like a sports car. David came to the door with a small bouquet of red and white roses. Out of the corner of her eye she saw a beautifully restored bright red sports car.

"Come in David, can I get you a drink before we go?" "Sure."

"What would you like?"

11

"A scotch and water will be fine."

She poured him a drink from the bar.

"Here you go."

Then she made the same for herself.

David said, "Gosh, I like your place. It's very impressive." "Please sit down and make yourself comfortable."

"I notice that you seem to have a lot of beautiful pieces. Have you been to all these places?"

"Not really, just some. I'm curious, where are we going for dinner?"

"I'll surprise you." David said.

"What did you do today, David?"

"Well, it looks like I acquired another apartment building which hopefully will be profitable."

She liked hearing about his real estate work and you could tell he really enjoyed it. They went to a charming little French restaurant in Palo Verdes. Their dinner was exquisite and David was impressive. He ordered everything in French.

They drank their drinks and enjoyed each other's company immensely. They seemed to have a lot in common. When they were ready to go, he was the perfect gentleman, helping her into her jacket and of course opening the car door for her.

When he took her home he said, "Donna I so glad that I finally got to meet you."

"Me too David."

"I would really like to get to get to know you better. Sometimes I get too busy."

"I know just what you mean. Me too."

"Could we do this again Donna? Maybe next weekend, is that too soon?"

"Not at all David."

He leaned down and gave her a light kiss on the mouth.

"I'll call you next week."

"Good night David."

Sheila called Donna the next day. Donna told her they had gone out.

"Okay, tell me all about it." Was he what you expected? "Yes Sheila, and more."

"When do you see him again?"

"Next weekend."

They went out again the next weekend on Saturday night. This time they went to an intimate Italian restaurant. The food was excellent and they had a good wine selection. They were taking their time enjoying their drinks.

David said, "Donna, you are certainly an independent woman. I like that. And needless to say, you probably make all your own business decisions too."

> "Well I try. Sometimes they are good and sometimes they are not so hot."

> "Have you ever been married?"

> "No, I have never had the courage."

> "Me neither. You know Sheila and Bob call us two free spirits. I think we are very much alike."

> "You may be right David."

When they said goodnight, David drew her to him and kissed her this time with a lot more tongue. Donna thought he was drop dead sexy and could hardly wait for what was next. He certainly didn't look like the bashful type.

> "Would you like to come in for a night cap or dessert, David?"

> "Yes, I would."

As they went into Donna's townhouse, she closed the front door. David drew her to him and gently pushed her against the wall. They began kissing again and she could feel him becoming aroused. His hand went under her blouse and he started to fondle her breasts. Then he started to undo her pants and move his hand between her legs. She could feel his fingers start to penetrate her and he started moving his erection against her. She started moaning softly and moving with him.

He said in a low and husky voice "Why don't we go into your bedroom?"

As they entered her bedroom, they quickly started removing each other's clothing. He was so hard she was having a difficult time with removing his pants.

> "David, maybe you should have your pants made with snaps and not a zipper. That might be easier."

With his help they managed to finally fall naked into her bed. Donna was on her back and David pushed her legs apart. He started kissing her breasts then moved his head down between her legs. She spread her legs even wider. She felt his tongue start to penetrate her, darting in slowly at first, then faster and faster, deeper and deeper. She was writhing with desire.

He kept this up until she cried out, "Now David, now!!"

He then moved his body upward against her and she felt his hardness against her body. She curled her fingers around his erection and he thrust himself deep inside her. She moaned loudly and he started moving deeper and deeper and faster and faster. Donna was undulating with desire and starting to lose control. She came once, then again until she cried out as she climaxed. David rolled over on his back and moved Donna on top of him. As she felt him start to enter her he grabbed her buttocks and thrust himself upward so his hardness went deep into her. She started to quicken the pace. They were both lost in the heat of passion, writhing with desire and simultaneously came to a climax. They both lay back panting hard and totally exhausted.

> "Well, David, I guess we don't need any dessert, do we?"

He gave a low chuckle, "It would have to be some dessert to beat what we just did to each other."

Donna invited David over for dinner the following week so he could meet her father. She wasn't much of a cook, but she liked a caterer close by and would have them deliver dinner. Donna's Dad was looking forward to it.

David loved talking to Don, Donna's father, and vice versa. Of course, the main topic of conversation was apartment buildings, but Donna didn't mind. She was used to it by now, listening to her father as she was growing up.

Donna and David enjoyed each other's company and they loved eating out, especially in all the ethnic restaurants in San Pedro. They also loved attending all the hit plays and musicals together, even sporting events if they could get good tickets.

During the day, they both worked diligently, Donna on her charity work and fund raising and David looking for neglected and run–down apartment buildings which he could turn around and sell at a good profit.

The relationship became more and more serious. It wasn't long before they were seeing each other almost every day.

David's father, John, could foresee a political future for his son, especially with his son's ongoing relationship becoming more and more serious with Donna Taylor. Donna was from a very well-known wealthy and prominent family in Southern California. They were always heavily involved in civic and community affairs. David was involved in real estate, specifically apartment buildings in the redevelopment areas. He liked to improve areas that had older and run-down apartments. David and his father met once a week for dinner. John was always bringing up the possibility of a political future for David, and he felt Donna would secure that possibility. David's father also knew his son liked his extracurricular activities with other women. Time after time he continually emphasized to David to be very discreet with his personal life. His father's encouragement about the politics began to sink in little by little and the more David thought about it the more he liked the idea. He started to date Donna on a more serious level and it didn't take long for their relationship to develop into a more permanent one.

One night at dinner, David brought up the topic of living together.

"Maybe we should move in together?"

Donna was quiet for a few minutes. She really liked her freedom and living by herself.

Reluctantly she said, "I guess we could try it for a while. I have plenty of room in my townhouse."

17

The co-habiting seemed to be working out better than she thought it would. David was kind and considerate and they had great sex. She loved having sex with him on a regular basis. He was a terrific lover and she couldn't get enough of his energy and stamina. On a scale of 1 to 10, he was off the charts. He was an exciting man and always wanted to please her and vice versa.

On one of their regular "Friday night date dinners"

David said "Donna, let's get married. Do you love me?" She said, "More than anything."

They had their fathers over for dinner who couldn't have been happier for them. They decided on a small and intimate wedding, just their fathers, Sheila and Bob, and a few close friends. Her father invited them to have the wedding at his estate in Palos Verdes in his lovely rose garden. He and Murphy, his boxer, would give Donna away. They all agreed. They would plan on a honeymoon sometime next year when they were not so busy.

After they were married, David's portfolio and bank account seemed to be growing by leaps and bounds.

> "Donna", he said, "I think we could use a bigger place. I think the time is right for it. What do you think?"

> "I think you are right David. Much as I love my townhouse, a bigger place might be better."

"I'll start looking in the area and see if I can find a place that might be in trouble and be a really good buy. The real estate market is way down and it's a great time to purchase something."

David came bursting in the door late one afternoon. He was excited.

"Honey, I think I found us a house! I am anxious for you to see it."

She said "Well, let's go, I can hardly wait. Tell me about it on the way."

"It's high on a hill in Palos Verdes on a large piece of land, and very spacious, with ocean and city views from almost every window. It has a large swimming pool and a very large deck which will be great for entertaining. There it is."

He pointed upward. David floored the accelerator and off they went up the driveway, all the way to the top. Donna's hand never let go of the door handle, just in case she needed to make a quick exit.

The owner, Ben Tyler, came out to greet them.

"Hi folks."

Introductions were made.

"Let me show you around."

He took them on a tour which took about 30 minutes. Donna was awestruck.

"I'll leave you two folks alone for a while and come back to see if you have any questions. Can I bring coffee or anything to drink for you when I come back?"

David said "No, we are okay, but thank you." David took Donna aside, "What do you think, Donna?"

"You know I'm impressed. I have a couple of concerns I would like you to bring up with the owner."

"I think I know what they are." "David, there is thick vegetation on one side of the house by the garage. Behind the vegetation there is no protection from a steep drop off to a ravine below. I think this is very unsafe. My other concern is that driveway, it is too steep."

"Let me talk to him about it."

"We have a couple of concerns Ben, the first is the unprotected side by the garage. We feel it is dangerous and very unsafe. Our other concern is the steep driveway. When we entertain, where will everyone park? We will need to have it leveled."

"I agree with you completely, David, on both of your concerns. I was going to put in a retaining wall before I sold it and also level the driveway. But my kids want me to move and be with them in Colorado as soon as I can."

20

David asked him, "Would you consider adjusting the purchase price to compensate for the retaining wall and leveling the steep driveway?"

"Yes, I would."

They negotiated for about half an hour and agreed on a final price. David went back to Donna.

"You're looking at our new house hon!"

Sheila stopped by one day to see David and Donna's new home. Donna opened the door to great her.

"Hi, I'm so glad you came by, Sheila. Let me walk you through, and I can make us some lunch afterwards."

Donna glanced out the window and saw Bob sitting in the car.

"Sheila, I didn't know that Bob was with you. For Pete's sake, ask him to come in."

Sheila broke up laughing.

"Ok, what's so funny Sheila?"

"That's not Bob, Donna, its Buster, our Rottweiler. You've got to get stronger glasses!!"

They both broke up. Everybody was always giving her a hard time about her eyesight, because she hardly ever wore her glasses. They had lunch and enjoyed each other's company. The wine was the best part of the lunch since Donna's cooking was not so memorable. As Sheila left she could hardly wait to get home and tell Bob he was looking more and more like Buster every day.

Once they were settled into their new home they invited her father, Don over for dinner. David and Don loved talking to each other about their real estate investments. After a while Donna said

> "Not to change the subject, guys, but after all this I need a break and am going to Catalina tomorrow for a couple of days."

> "David, will you tell me what she sees in that place? There is a casino with no gambling, a bird sanctuary with no birds, a prison with no prisoners, fish that fly, and a 3rd Street with no 1st, 2nd, or 4th Streets."

> "Don, you got me, I have no idea. I can't explain it."

> "Look guys, it's the one thing I do for myself several times a year. It's a girl thing. I need to get away from my work and just shop, shop, shop."

Don always brought Murphy, his loveable boxer with him to Donna's. Murphy, as far as they were concerned, was family. The one thing that kind of bothered Donna was she noticed Murphy seemed to tolerate David. He didn't go nuts over him like he did with Sheila and Bob. Murphy was always a pretty good thermometer when it came to judging people. Maybe it would take a little time. Donna thought she better get back to her guests so she put it on the back burner for now.

David and Donna had been in their new house for a few months and were constantly making changes. Donna had hoped that David would have the retaining wall put in by now. She hated to bug him about it. He always seemed to get side tracked about something or other. She knew it would eventually get done but she wished it was sooner rather than later. It worried her. She decided to bring it to his attention one more time.

> "David, until that retaining wall is put in could we at least put up a barricade and some appropriate signs like Danger, Private Property. No Trespassing? Just as a precaution? What do you think?"

> "Good idea hon. I'll take care of it right away."

David then called his workers and told them to put up a barricade with the warning signs. Then he told them he wanted a retaining wall put in when they had clearer weather. You can bring up the materials you need anytime and cover them until the rain has stopped.

He thought, this should make Donna happy.

Once in a while Donna would turn on the TV early in the morning just to catch up on the news. Unfortunately, the media was always rattling on about some well-known celebrity or politician that was carrying on a torrid affair with some young thing. She really didn't want to listen to this; it sounded more like a soap opera or gossip rather than news. Thank goodness she and David were happily married. She didn't give it a second thought.

CHAPTER 6

In her youth, Sandy Grant had been bounced around from one foster home to another. It's a good thing Sandy was very skinny and unattractive growing up because it worked to her advantage. There were horror stories about foster homes being abusive to children. However, she was a late bloomer and at sixteen her figure began to fill out and she started to blossom into a beautiful young girl. Her last foster home wasn't as bad as the others because she could at least attend a school close by. She became close friends with Alecia, a girl her own age at the school and her family. One day her foster home told her they would have to give her up. They had gone broke, and she would be sent to another home soon. Sandy couldn't stop crying and called Alecia, telling her the bad news. Alecia was just as upset as Sandy and her father heard his daughter crying. He picked up the phone from Alecia and Sandy told him what had happened. She would have to leave soon.

Alecia's father said "No you don't have to. You're coming to live with our family. Pack your things now and we will pick you up in fifteen minutes."

She packed quickly without telling anyone at the home and left when Alecia came with her father to get her. She loved their family and they made her feel at home, like she was part of their family. Sandy was able to continue her schooling and excelled at business and secretarial skills.

After graduating high school, she enrolled in a nearby junior college and majored in business. She worked as a secretary part time to help pay for her schooling. She met and fell in love with one of the salesmen at work and they were eventually married. They both loved the ocean and had always talked about moving to Southern California near the water. About five years later a job opportunity came up for him in the Marina del Rey area and they moved there. She kept in touch with Alecia and her family after the move. She would always be grateful for them. Unfortunately, Sandy's husband was killed in a car accident a few years later. She was devastated when she lost her husband. He was a good man and she missed him terribly. In the event of his death, he had left Sandy a $200,000 life insurance policy, which he thought at the time she might need someday. She did, and needed a car desperately, which she could pay cash for with some of the insurance money. The rest she put in the bank. One day at work someone told her about a little 34' power boat that was for sale. Curious, she went to look at it and liked it immediately. The owner gave her a good price and she used some of the insurance money again to pay all cash for it. She bought it on the condition that he would show her how to operate it. She was a fast learner and it was hers in no time. He told her eventually that she might like to move it to a marina further south near the San Pedro area. The slip fees were a lot lower there and he thought that she would enjoy the colorful atmosphere especially in San Pedro.

She called a marina manager in the San Pedro area, a Jim Porter, and introduced herself.

> "Jim, I currently have a 34' boat in Marina del Rey. I would like to move it to your marina and live aboard it. Do you have anything available?"

> "Yes, I do. I have a good spot that will be available shortly. It is on gangway 15, slip 4."

She said that she would like to drive down and see it as soon as possible. They set up a time for the very next day.

Sandy drove her little Toyota down to the marina to meet Jim Porter. She had never been to San Pedro before and was looking forward to it. She met with Jim and he couldn't have been nicer. He gave her a little walking tour and showed her the space coming up on gangway 15. Sandy asked him about the security and safety there. He said that it was good and that they hadn't had any incidents.

> "Tell me about the owners of the boats that would be on each side of me."

> "Both have been here for quite a few years, Sandy. They are middle aged and very friendly. I think that you will like them quite a lot. I'll introduce you to both owners if you decide you want the space."

"Oh, would it be possible to have a space close by for my car? It's a little Toyota Corolla."

"Absolutely."

"Is there any charge for that?"

"No there isn't, and it's a secured space."

"Also, this is my first boat I have ever owned. I would feel more comfortable if someone could bring it down from Marina del Rey to your marina for me. Could you recommend someone? I would be glad to pay them for their time."

"Yes, I do Sandy. They work with me here and are very reliable and do this quite often when we have someone new moving in."

They set up a time and date for the move next week and she signed the papers.

"Jim, I'm going to grab a quick lunch, I'll be back in about an hour. That will give me a little more time to see if I have any more questions."

"Sounds good Sandy."

"I saw a place down the way called "The Wharf". Is that pretty good?"

"Yes, it is. The bartender's name is Charlie. He's a good guy and can recommend something good for lunch."

"Can I bring you back anything Jim, a sandwich perhaps?"

"No, I brown bagged it today, but thank you Sandy."

27

"Okay, see you soon."

"You bet."

Sandy decided to walk to "The Wharf" which took her all of ten minutes. She sat at the bar and the bartender came over immediately. She noticed the "Charlie" nametag on his shirt.

> "Charlie, my name is Sandy. I'm new around here and am moving my little boat down soon. Jim at the marina said that you could recommend something good for lunch."

> "Well Sandy, it will be nice to have a pretty face around here for a change. How about an ice-cold beer to cool you off first and then one of our hot pastrami sandwiches with a dill pickle?"

> "That sounds perfect."

He brought the beer right away in a frosted mug and the sandwich a little later.

> "Charlie, this sandwich is delicious."

He smiled and said, "I'm glad you like it Sandy."

When she was done she said, "Charlie, see you soon."

> "Looking forward to having you here Sandy. When do you think you'll have your boat here?"

> "Probably by next week."

> "See you then."

> "Hurry back," Charlie said.

Sandy Grant had her small boat moved from Marina Del Rey to the San Pedro Harbor, within a week. She liked the idea she could keep her reliable Toyota close to her boat. Sandy loved the area and felt she could afford it with the secretarial work she had recently found close by. Little by little she became familiar with the local bars and small restaurants that she could conveniently walk to from her boat. Perhaps if she was lucky she could meet some new men. She still liked "The Wharf" the best. The drinks and the appetizers were very good and reasonable. It seemed like a great place to socialize and Charlie was the best bartender around.

David had been in the San Pedro Harbor area looking at a couple of rundown apartment buildings for investments. It was getting a little late in the afternoon and he was tired and thirsty. He thought he would call it a day. As he was going to his car he saw The Wharf Bar & Grill sign.

He thought, I could sure use a beer right now. He headed over. The Wharf was a small and cozy place and had a great bar. There was a large mirror on the back wall facing the bar stools. You could sit at the bar and actually see who came in and who went out. Sandy was sitting at the bar having a drink and looked up at the mirror and saw a very tall, attractive man come in. The only bar stool available was one over from Sandy's. He sat down there.

Charlie, the bartender came over, "Hi there, what can I get for you?"

"An ice-cold beer sounds great. Hot day today."

Charlie brought him a large beer in a frosty mug with some peanuts.

"I haven't seen you in here before."

"I was in the area doing some business and this looked like the place to be."

"Right on." Charlie was a friendly guy.

David glanced in the large mirror across the bar and did a double take. There was a woman sitting a seat over from him that looked exactly like his wife. Incredible, they could easily be twins, she also had the same thick blonde hair and looked very shapely. When the seat next to her became available, David leaned over and said to her, "Mind if I move over?"

"No, not at all."

They introduced each other and started talking about things in general.

"Do you live around here, Sandy?"

"Yes, I have a small boat down the way. I can just walk here. What about you?"

"I live just a few miles away."

He motioned to Charlie to bring her another drink.

"Thank you, David. What were you doing down here?"

"I was looking at some property for investment and got thirsty."

He ordered another beer.

"One for the road Charlie, and put another drink for Sandy on my tab."

"Thank you again David."

"Unfortunately, Sandy, I have to leave in a few minutes but I'll be back next week. Maybe I'll see you then."

"I hope so." she said.

"Have a good evening Sandy."

"You too." She did notice that he had a ring on his finger and thought, It never fails, why does this always happen with the nice ones?

David ran into Sandy a couple more times. He knew that he was attracted to her and could feel the attraction between them.

The third time, Sandy said "Let me buy you a drink for a change."

"You don't have to do that."

"I know but I want to."

"Thank you."

"What kind of week did you have Sandy?"

"Well, I was busy and I have a couple of annoying little problems on my boat that are driving me crazy."

31

"I'm pretty handy, Sandy. I can take a look and see if I can fix them for you."

"Oh, I don't mean to impose."

"No problem Sandy. Next week I will take a look. Would 3:00 in the afternoon be good for you?"

"You bet."

"My boat is on gangway 15, slip 4. The name is Sandy's Getaway."

When he left, he said "See you next week."

The next week, David spotted "Sandy's Getaway" right away.

"Hello, Hello I'm here."

"Hi, David. Come on down below."

He went below.

"I like this Sandy. This looks like you."

You could tell it had a woman's touch.

"Show me what you're concerned about."

They moved to the little kitchen area.

"As you can see, these kitchen cabinets are not closing properly." David examined them.

"No problem there, Sandy. What else?"

"I have some electrical problems with a few of these appliances."

"Ok, I can fix those. What else?"

32

"The lamp on my nightstand keeps flickering."

"Let's see."

They went into her bedroom. He sat on her bed and worked with the light switch.

"Okay, I can take care of these things for you. I'll bring my tool kit next time."

God, he was gorgeous, what a hunk, she thought.

"Anything else you need?"

"I think that's it David. Thank you so much."

"Well then I guess I'd better be going."

She noticed he was having difficulty standing up. When he finally got up she noticed a very large bulge beneath his belt buckle.

"David, I really don't think we should let that go to waste."

He couldn't take his clothes off fast enough. Sandy did the same. They fell together on the bed naked and she could feel his hardness pressing against her body. His hand started moving down her thighs and she spread her legs apart. She felt his fingers begin to penetrate her. She began to moan softly, moving her body up and down. He slid one finger in and then two inside her. His fingers started moving in and out slowly at first then faster and faster. He moved up and she felt his erection coming between her legs. He thrust himself easily into her wetness harder and deeper. He began moving faster and

33

faster until she was writhing with desire. He was driving her insane.

She cried out, "Don't stop, David. Don't stop."

She wrapped her legs around his waist. He thrust himself into her again and again deeper and deeper until she cried out and came over and over again. He then moved her on top of him. She lowered herself easily onto his hardness and he thrust himself upward until he was even deeper inside her. She started riding him faster and harder and harder until she was completely out of control. In the heat of passion they both simultaneously came to a climax.

Sandy and David lay back totally exhausted. They rested until it was time for David to leave.

"David, you were incredible."

"You too," he said. Sandy said, "I hope to see you soon, David."

"Well, I'll be back next week, I still have business here. I'll look for you at The Wharf."

She could hardly wait. She hoped her body could. When David left, his legs were a little wobbly but he made it back to his car at The Wharf.

They continued to meet twice a week for the next six months. The last time he left she put an envelope in his jacket pocket when he wasn't looking.

When David was driving home, he stopped at a stop sign and felt something in the pocket of his jacket. He didn't remember putting anything there. Curious, he pulled it out. It was an open envelope. He looked inside and saw naked photos of Sandy in suggestive poses. Good grief! He thought why did she do this?!! He almost hit the car in front of him. Then the car in back of him started beeping his horn loudly. Holy cow, he could have had a bad accident. He pulled over to the side of the street. He was sweating and started to panic. He was almost home. He quickly slipped the envelope under the driver's seat. Thank God Donna had her own car and never took his pickup. This thing with Sandy was getting out of control. He had to do something about this. Enough is enough! He could easily find more action elsewhere. It was time for him to move on and find something new to play with. The warning signs had been there, but as they say, he had waited too long to jump ship.

When David saw her the next week he said

> "Sandy we have to end this now. I don't know what happened. It was fun while it lasted, but it's over."

> "So apparently this meant nothing to you."

> "That's right, Sandy. Just forget it."

When he left, Sandy started crying. He was so nice and she loved having him make love to her. She thought they were becoming more and more serious. She knew she would miss him terribly. The following days became longer and longer. She became more depressed and very lonely.

Donna was in a hurry to meet with the director of the fund raiser for a late Friday afternoon meeting. Why were Fridays always so hectic? As she left the house she noticed David's pick-up truck in the driveway. She remembered he had taken his car that morning to have it serviced. She hurried to her car and punched the ignition. Nothing- dead silence. She thought, "It's probably a dead battery." She didn't have time to call the Auto Club. She ran back to the house to find the extra key for his pickup. She didn't want to be late. Luckily, she found the key and ran out to start it.

> "Oh, hell she said out loud. I can't reach the pedals."

She reached for the adjuster under the seat and felt a small paper package. She pulled it out. It was an open envelope. Curious she looked inside. They were photos of a naked woman in various suggestive poses. Donna sat there in shock, paralyzed, unable to move. Ironically, she and the woman looked very much alike. They actually could be twins. She knew at that moment their marriage was over. She would never be able to trust him again.

Feeling nauseous, she went back to the house and called the director of the foundation, Arthur.

> "I woke up with the flu this morning, Arthur, and cannot make our meeting this afternoon."

> "Donna that's okay. Just take care of yourself."

Friday's were always Donna and David's "special date night". They always celebrated it by going to one of their favorite restaurants. She knew he would be home soon. She sat there in the dark in the study waiting for him. She heard the door open.

> "Hi honey, I'm starving. Where are we going to dinner tonight?"

He came into the study.

> "Hi gorgeous, why are you sitting in the dark?"

She flung the photos at him. Screaming,

> "Who in the fuck is this David?!!"

Oh my God, David just stood there his face ashen. She found the photos!!

> "Donna, you know I love you more than anything. This meant nothing. It's over. Donna I am so sorry."

> "Don't you dare say that!!" she yelled.

> "It was a very bad mistake, Donna."

> "I can't tell you what a surprise I had today, David. My car has a dead battery and I was going to use your pick-up. What a shock when I adjusted the driver's seat!! God damn you! How could you do this to us?"

David said, "I never meant to hurt you like this."

> "It's a little late for hindsight David. I thought we had a good life together. Didn't I love you enough? Wasn't I always there for you? I WANT

YOU OUT OF THIS HOUSE!! NOW!! I can't stand
the sight of you. JUST GO, GET OUT NOW!!"

"I'll call you tomorrow Donna. We need to talk
about this."

She said, "WHO CARES? I REALLY DON'T GIVE A
SHIT."

The next day Donna called her best friend, Sheila. She had
to talk to someone. Sheila answered the phone,

"Hello."

"Hi Sheila, this is Donna."

"Donna, this doesn't sound like you. Are you
okay?"

"Not really Sheila, I need to talk to someone.
Something awful has happened. Can you meet me
for lunch today?"

"Of course. Why don't you come here Donna?
Bob is in a golf tournament all day."

"Thank you, is 12:00 a good time Sheila?"

"Absolutely. See you then."

When Donna arrived Sheila could tell she had been
crying. She could see the pain and hurt in Donna's eyes.
Donna told her what had happened. Sheila couldn't
believe it and was in shock.

"How could David do this to you?"

"I don't know Sheila. I'll never figure it out. He was the love of my life and I thought I was his. You think you know someone, but sometimes you never do. He spent a lot of time looking at properties, Sheila. I thought they were all buildings, but I guess not. I was so clueless."

When she and David split her father had never seen her so unhappy.

> "I'm worried about you honey. Can I help with anything?"

> "No Dad. I'll get over this in time."

He knew how she felt. He was very fond of David, too. They had a lot in common and Don would miss him. He had an inkling of what might have happened, but Donna would tell him if she wanted him to know. Don knew his daughter well and he knew this was the end of their marriage. Donna's pencil never did have an eraser.

> "Ok baby, I remember how happy you were in your townhouse before you met David. Why don't I scout around for another place like that for you? It would probably be a good idea for you to eventually sell this house when everything is finalized. It's too big for you and too many bad memories now."

> "You know Dad; you always know what is best for me. I would like that."

CHAPTER 7

Donna couldn't seem to get herself together. She couldn't think clearly after the split with David. She decided to seek professional help. A friend referred her to Dr. Bill Townsend, a psychiatrist, who was close by at a large medical facility. Donna made an appointment with him and went to his office. His secretary said he would be with her in a few minutes.

"Can I get you some coffee or anything to drink Mrs. Collins?"

"No thank you, I'm fine."

When he came out she was surprised. He was not what she expected. He was probably in his early forties and very good looking. She thought he would be a lot older, with glasses, balding and shorter. He introduced himself and said,

"Mrs. Collins please come in my office."

She sat down across from him and he said, "Tell me a little bit about yourself, Mrs. Collins."

He was pleasant and she started to relax and feel better.

Dr. Townsend was born and educated in Portland, Oregon. His father had threatened to cut him out of his will if he didn't go to work and make something of himself. Bill never seemed to have any motivation to work but he loved being a professional student. Bill went on to get his PhD in mental health and could have made a very good living as a psychiatrist or a professor with his excellent qualifications if he wanted to. His father kept after him to find a good job. One day Bill was getting sick and tired of his father hounding him. An ad in the newspaper caught his eye for a position as a psychiatrist with a major clinic in Southern California. The facility was in a prime location and close to the ocean. He sent his resume and was surprised to receive an e-mail from them the very next day asking him if he could come by for an interview as soon as possible, all expenses paid. He replied immediately.

They arranged a date and time and Bill flew to Los Angeles. When he arrived, he rented a car and went to the hotel they reserved for him. He unpacked, had an early dinner in his room and mentally prepared for the interview the next morning.

He thought the interview went very well, and the director introduced him to the other staff members. When he left, the director seemed pleased and said they would get back to him soon. Bill did not see any reason to mention to the director that he had a brother, Paul, with a major drug problem. He lived in a facility that allowed patients to live there on a permanent basis. Bill had never told

41

anyone about his brother. He thought it would reflect badly on him and it really didn't seem that important.

Bill knew his father would leave the bulk of his estate to Paul, who was his youngest son. This always pissed off Bill but there was nothing he could do about it. His father had helped with his education and he felt that was enough. He knew Bill could always take care of himself. Hell, if he didn't want to practice psychiatry he could at least teach it. But Bill didn't want to do either. Bill was basically lazy and was always looking or scheming for the easy way out to make money. His good looks had helped him many times. He knew women liked him so he focused on the ones with money.

When he returned home from California, the director called him the next day. The position was his. He was surprised to hear from them so soon. They were anxious for him to start right away. Bill was on his way. He had researched the area where he would be practicing ahead of time. He was impressed with the amount of wealth there. What a great opportunity for him. He could visualize women coming in droves to him for help with their problems. He could hardly wait. Things were looking up. This was going to work out even better than he expected.

Bill was very handsome and charismatic. Women were always telling him he looked like a movie star that was on television. They were always coming on to him and he loved it.

Before Bill knew it, he had been at the facility almost a year. The women patients adored him, mainly because of his good looks and the attention he showered on them. Little did they know he had ulterior motives. He was a predator of wealthy women and should be avoided at all costs.

Donna felt comfortable talking to Dr. Townsend and told him everything about her privileged life, affluent family, her marriage to David, his affair and her work with charities and fund raising.

He said, "I am so glad you came to me Mrs. Collins. I can tell how hard things have been for you and it was probably very difficult for you to come here."

He told her a little about his background, where he was from, education, etc. Donna was infatuated with him from the start.

"Mrs. Collins please allow an hour for each session. Does that sound satisfactory to you? At the end of the month we will go over what you have accomplished and any concerns you still have. Here is my card with all my numbers. Feel free to call me anytime. Mrs. Collins, after all you have been through I think we should start with our sessions twice a week. An hour for each session. How does that sound to you?"

"I think that would be very helpful doctor."

"Good, my secretary will set up the dates and time with you before you leave today."

After two months Dr. Townsend asked,

> "Mrs. Collins do you think our sessions twice a week are starting to help?"

> "Yes, I do."

> "I noticed that you seem more at ease and a lot calmer now."

> "Yes, I think so."

> "I was thinking that just for a change of pace we could meet for lunch as part of our appointments. Would you like that?"

> "Yes, I would."

> "Very well, next week instead of meeting here, I will meet you at the same time but at the Breaker's 9 restaurant. Is that okay?"

> "Yes, I'll look forward to it."

Next week they met at Breaker's 9.

Dr. Townsend said, "Mrs. Collins let's have a drink to celebrate. What would you like?"

> "A very dry martini with two olives sounds good."

He gave the waiter her order and he said, "I'll have a scotch and water. I would feel more comfortable if you called me Bill, if that's alright with you."

> "Of course."

They clinked glasses.

> "May I call you Donna?"

44

"Yes, you may."

They discussed Donna's usual concerns over their drinks before ordering.

"Let's have another, Donna. We are in no hurry here and not on any schedule. I think we have a lot to celebrate."

She said, "You know this is one of my favorite restaurants. Do they have eight others?"

"No, only this one. I heard the owner say nine is his lucky number."

The second round of drinks came and Bill moved to a more personal level.

"So, Donna, I am amazed how a woman by herself can take care of so many properties?"

She told him.

"Good grief, it's a wonder you're not exhausted. How many apartments do you actually have?"

"About five of varying sizes."

"And then there is that big house you have."

"Well, thank goodness I have a staff of people to help with the cleaning, landscaping and gardening."

"I don't know how you do it, Donna, you're very impressive. I know that you are separated now. Are you considering reconciling with your husband or more of a permanent split?"

45

"I am in the process of filing for a divorce now."

"I think that is a wise choice for you Donna."

Bill was thinking to himself "What is that silly expression? I believe I have met the goose that laid the golden egg."

Their lunch sessions started becoming longer and longer and moving into the dinner hour. They became more and more personal. The relationship was moving from a casual one to a more serious one. Bill's sexual prowess in the bedroom left a lot to be desired, but at this stage of the game Donna thought she would overlook it. Donna was a very physical as well as mental person and she was used to men who were the same. Maybe things would change later in the sexual department with Bill but she had her reservations. She could estimate their lovemaking in minutes rather than in hours from what she was used to. She noticed that her father and close friends, Sheila and Bob, did not seem overjoyed with the relationship.

Donna's father, Don asked Donna to join him for dinner. He needed to clear up some things regarding her personal life. He wanted to start out on the right foot so he took her to one of her favorite restaurants. They ordered drinks before deciding what they wanted for dinner.

> "Honey, I know this break-up with David has been hard for you, but I wanted to know if everything is working out with Dr. Townsend? Is he helping? It seems like you are seeing more and more of him."

> "Oh Dad."

Donna was being unresponsive.

"I was just curious. I know he's not married and it's quite natural for patients to become attracted to their doctors."

"Dad don't be silly."

"I know but I just worry about you. I don't want you jumping into anything too soon."

"I won't Dad. Let's talk about something else."

CHAPTER 8

David was trying very hard to save their marriage but reconciliation was out of the question for Donna. One morning as she was fixing herself coffee she heard David's car come up the driveway. When he came to the door she said, "David, I have filed for divorce with my lawyer and he will be contacting you."

"Donna, couldn't we talk this out?"

"There is nothing to talk about."

David said "A divorce will put one hell of a dent in our assets."

"It's a little late for hindsight David, you should have thought of that before. You know I really can't stand the sight of you anymore. I need to get on with my life now. Maybe the next time around I'll be luckier and meet a guy who can keep his dick in his pants. The sooner you are out of here the better!! Please leave now!!"

As a last resort, David said, "Maybe we should see a marriage counselor."

"I don't think a counselor can cure your dick problem David. Apparently that's what you have been thinking with."

48

Donna met with Irv, her attorney, to ask some additional questions regarding the divorce. "Irv, if I'm seeing someone else since David and I split, would this affect any of the settlement before the divorce is final?"

"No that would not be a problem since David was the cause of the split and the divorce."

She said "What if who I was seeing moved in with me before the divorce was final?"

"I would not go that far until after the divorce is finalized. David could always say you were also having an affair."

Donna was familiar with all five of the apartments they owned. She told Irv she wanted the house and specifically which apartment buildings she wanted. Irv said that he would put all of it in the settlement and discuss this with David's attorney. As far as monies and other investments, Donna thought she was entitled to a high percentage since she was not the one having the affair. She asked Irv, "Why in the hell do divorces take so long?"

"I guess there's a chance of reconciliation if someone changes their mind."

"Fat chance. I don't think so Irv."

David's attorney, John Black, called him and told him he had the final divorce settlement ready. David went in sat down, read it and had a fit.

"Good grief John, Donna's taking me to the cleaners!!"

"Can't I do any better than this?"

"I'm afraid not David. You were the guilty party."

"John, for Christ's sake, you know most guys do this sort of thing."

"I know David, but you got caught with your "pants down" so to speak."

David thought "It was those damn photos that did it!!" David left his attorney's office very depressed and angry. "How in the hell was he ever going to recover from this?" It was going to be a long road to get even remotely back to where he was before.

David couldn't believe how his life had changed. It went from a great one to into the dumpster in a very short time. Sandy had ruined his marriage. If it hadn't been for those damn photos everything would be the same. Donna would have never known the difference. Not only was their marriage shot, but he lost more than half of his properties he had worked so hard on in the divorce settlement, plus the house they lived in. Donna had no interest at all in reconciliation. A reconciliation would have solved all his problems, but that was out of the question for Donna.

David thought, Donna had certainly wasted no time starting a new relationship. He was really pissed off when one of his friends had seen Donna at Breaker's 9 with a very nice-looking guy.

His friend told him, "They looked like they were enjoying each other's company and were being very affectionate toward each other."

Women, he just didn't understand them. Things happen; this little affair meant nothing to him. Women take things way too seriously. He should never have had sex with Sandy. What a mistake it was and it was a whopper. It was fun while it lasted, but she was getting much too serious, and it had to stop. It had cost him dearly, his marriage and a very serious dent in his net worth. Especially with the loss of his properties he had worked so hard on. Donna had her pick of the apartments in the divorce settlement. She was smart and she knew what properties had the most upside. His other big problem was how in the hell he was going to explain all of this to his father, John. His father would consider this extreme foolishness. After all, a large portion of his loss was his father's too. John had trusted him and backed him monetarily. David didn't think he would be so magnanimous again.

David finally got up enough nerve to tell his Dad what happened. John threw a fit.

> "Couldn't you have been more discreet for God's sake?"

> "I thought I was, but it was those damn photos"

> "Now, you're going to have to start all over again."

> "I know, Dad and I'm sorry."

> "What do you think I am, a goddamn money tree?"

And that was that. David left on that note more depressed and upset than ever.

CHAPTER 9

Donna knew she had to get involved with the apartments as soon as possible. She had to admit she was afraid. She had never dealt with people like this. Many of them were on welfare and some of them were druggies and could not hold down a job for any length of time. A few even had rap sheets a mile long, and some had even been in prison for felonies and miscellaneous crimes.

David had warned her, "Donna you won't be able to manage these apartments. You don't know what kind of people you'll be dealing with."

But she was determined. He had underestimated her. By God, she would show him.

Donna knew she had to hire some kind of protection. Donna had a lot of friends in important positions. She called her good friend Joe Evans at the city hall in San Pedro. Joe was in administration and she had his direct number. He knew everybody in San Pedro. She knew he would be able to help her. Natalie, his secretary answered his phone.

"Joe Evans' office."

"Hi Natalie, this is Donna. How are you?"

"Great stranger."

"Natalie, is Joe available?"

"Yes, he's around here somewhere causing trouble as usual. Hold on a minute."

Joe came on the line.

"Is this my good friend that only calls when she needs something?"

"Hi Joe, this is Donna. I need a big favor."

She explained her situation to him.

"Well you're in luck Donna. I have just the right person for you. His name is Ivan. Scary as hell, and believe me you won't be disappointed. I'll give you his number and tell him you'll be calling him right away."

"Joe, I can't thank you enough."

"You know, Donna, you'll owe me big time for this, a fancy dinner and drinks."

"You got it Joe. Bye-bye."

When Donna thought Joe had had enough time to call Ivan, she called him.

"Hi Ivan, this is Donna. Did Joe give you a call?"

"Oh, hi Donna, yes he did."

"Did he tell you what I needed?"

"Yes, he did."

"Oh, good Ivan. I was thinking perhaps we could meet for coffee and I can tell you more of the details."

"Okay."

"Are you familiar with Curly's Bar & Grill in San Pedro right across from the post office?"

"I am."

"Can you meet me there today at 3:00?"

"Sounds good, Donna."

"See you then Ivan."

When Donna arrived at Curly's she saw a big black Harley parked in front. "Bet I know who that belongs to." she thought. She recognized Ivan immediately when she walked in. He was sitting in a back booth facing the door. He stood up when she approached.

"Hi Donna."

"Hi Ivan."

Ivan had a head of thick black hair, was huge and looked very muscular. He looked very physically fit. He was dressed all in black from his leather jacket all the way down to his big black boots. He wore heavy gold chains around his thick neck and a pierced gold earring in one ear. She didn't see any other piercings at least not on the outside. When he smiled at her something shiny caught Donna's eye. It was a gold tooth right in front. Damn she thought, I should have worn more jewelry.

Darlene, the waitress, hustled over to the booth snapping her gum.

> "Hi I'm Darlene, your waitress today. What can I get for the two of you?"

She was in her early forties. Her bright red hair was piled high on her head like one of those old-fashioned beehives and a little yellow ribbon stuck out of one side of her hair. Darlene's tight fitting skimpy black uniform proudly displayed lots of cleavage. Donna said, "I'm just going to have a cup of coffee Darlene. Ivan what would you like?" Darlene's eyes lit up when she looked at Ivan.

> "Darlene, I would like a cup of hot chocolate with whipped cream if you have it? I really like whipped cream."

Darlene grinned and winked at him.

> "I like whipped cream too, Ivan."

When she brought the drinks, she set Ivan's down in front of him and leaned way over exposing her ample cleavage even more. "Honey, I gave you an extra big cup with lots and lots of whipped cream."

> "Thank you, Darlene." he winked back at her.

Donna glanced nervously at the crowded bar to see if anyone was noticing Ivan with his hot chocolate and whipped cream. She thought if anyone messes with this guy they're in a world of trouble. Ivan began to relax a little more and removed his big black leather jacket.

Darlene and Donna both couldn't help staring at his bulging muscles beneath his tight-fitting black t-shirt.

Donna thought "He's perfect. Good grief, the top of him is massive and his arms are as big as the top of my legs. He makes a very scary statement."

Donna could see the mutual attraction between Ivan and Darlene. She didn't want the conversation to get sidetracked so Donna spoke up. "I hate to break this up but we need to discuss a few things Ivan."

Darlene excused herself. Donna went over what Ivan's responsibilities would be and what she expected of him. She also mentioned the starting salary and possibility of advancement. "What do you think Ivan? Do you have any questions for me?"

"No, I'm good to go Donna."

He seemed pleased. She then gave him a list of the names of the tenants in each apartment.

"I want you to be my protector and enforcer Ivan." She thought to herself, IVAN THE ENFORCER, I like the sound of that.

When they got up to leave, Darlene came over to personally say goodbye especially to Ivan.

"See you big guy. Come back real soon."

She gave him a winning smile swinging her hips as she sashayed back to her other customers.

The tenants in Donna's apartments saw the change immediately in the management. The minute Donna took over the management from David she became an easy mark. They could hardly wait to play their little games and take advantage of her. Leo Garcia was one of the worst trouble makers.

He said "It will be fun to see what we can get away with. Especially with this bitch."

However, when the tenants caught their first glimpse of Ivan, the Enforcer, the situation with the tenant's games did a one hundred and eighty degree turn around. Especially when they realized that he was a permanent fixture of the management. This was the first "real" job Ivan had ever had and he felt like a different person. He loved working for Donna and would do anything for her. He was feeling so good that he might even give Darlene a call at Curly's to see if she would like to share some whipped cream with him tonight.

Donna thought Ivan was working out perfectly. He had even changed her attitude. She had become thick skinned with Ivan always right beside her. She was no longer afraid of the tenants. If she had to evict a tenant for causing trouble or back rent she had no problem with throwing out all their belongings in the back alley by the trash if they didn't leave right away. Their locks would also be changed right away. She knew that legally she didn't have a leg to stand on but she didn't give a damn! These people had pushed her to the limit! She was surprised she had never received any legal repercussions from any of the tenants. She realized of course, that Ivan, the Enforcer, might have been an influencing factor. He made a very scary statement indeed.

Ivan had fifteen biker buddies and five new recruits. They not only helped each other out in times of trouble, but others as well. They also had an excellent reputation as independent contractors. They were known for their workmanship, fairness and honesty. Because of their massive size and tremendous strength, they were able to do a variety of jobs which may have been difficult or even impossible for the average worker. Consequently, they were able to make a very comfortable living and live the lifestyle they wanted.

Originally Donna had thought about selling the apartments when the time was right. However, she had second thoughts when she saw how much their property values had improved over such a short time. The right management, thanks to Ivan, had helped immensely to contribute to their net worth and so far, she was content to keep them. Donna's father was delighted. He was so proud of her and loved seeing a part of himself in her since he had made his fortune in apartment investments. Don thought his daughter was definitely a "chip off the old block".

Donna couldn't believe how well Ivan was working out. She was thinking about hiring him full time. He certainly didn't need her tagging along any longer by his side. She called her father to ask him what he thought. Don was at home when Donna called. He picked up the phone right away. "Hi sweetie, what can I do for you?"

"Dad, I'd like to run something by you in regard to my apartments."

"Sure thing. Why don't you come over here and have a bite of lunch?"

He loved it when she wanted advice or whatever.

A few minutes later Murphy, his boxer, heard her car in the driveway and could hardly wait to greet her at the door. It took about ten minutes for him to settle down before Donna could talk to her Dad.

"Hon, I made us some tuna mango sandwiches and some soup for lunch. How does that sound?"

"Great Dad. You know that is my favorite sandwich."

"Do you want a soft drink or glass of wine?"

"Just a soft drink."

"Now, what's on your mind?"

They sat down in his study and she told him how well Ivan was working out.

"I'd like to hire him full time Dad. I feel he can handle all the buildings by himself."

"You know, I think that is an excellent idea. And it will give you more time to spend with your charity work or going to Catalina."

"Oh, Dad, I'm so glad you think so. I'll do it right away. Let's have lunch, I'm starved."

When she left her Dad's, Donna called Ivan from her cell phone in the car.

Ivan picked up, "Hi Donna. What's up?"

"Ivan, I have good news for you that I think you might like. I'll be in San Pedro in about fifteen minutes. Can you meet me at Curly's?"

"Of course, Donna, see you there."

When Donna walked into Curly's she saw Ivan sitting at the back booth where they originally met. He always stood up when he saw her walk in. Darlene, the waitress came running over to their table to serve them.

"Okay guys, what sounds good today? Hot chocolate and whipped cream for the big guy?"

"You bet Darlene."

Donna said, "I'll just have coffee. Ivan, how about some pie or a sandwich? Have you had lunch?"

"I'm okay Donna, but a piece of apple pie sounds great." Darlene scurried off with their order.

"Ivan," Donna said, "I'm so pleased with your work at the apartments."

"Thank you, Donna."

"I would like to offer you the job full time with full benefits including vacation time of course, and a substantial increase in pay. What do you think?"

"I think I would love it Donna."

"I am so glad you feel that way Ivan."

They discussed salary and Donna could tell from Ivan's expression he was more than pleased. They agreed on the salary, and Donna said that she would have all the details written up and given to him.

"I will also order personal business cards to be printed for you right away. And Ivan, you know I will always be available for you if you have any questions. Do we have a deal?"

Ivan gave her a broad smile, his front gold tooth glistening.

"Yes, we do Donna, and thank you again."

"As of today, Ivan, you're my property manager and I think you'll be the best in town."

Darlene brought their drinks and pie for Ivan. Donna was so happy, she could hardly wait to tell her father.

When Donna got in her car to go home, she called her Dad immediately from her cell phone and told him what happened. Don was very pleased.

She said, "I'm going to have to write down his plan and would like to have you approve it to make sure I have covered everything for him."

"Just let me know hon."

Don loved it when she asked for his advice. He could hear the excitement in her voice. He thought, That's my girl.

When Donna had Ivan's formal full-time job information printed out with all the specifics, hours, salary, vacation, benefits, etc., she went to her father to have him take a look at it. Don thought it looked good and actually didn't have any suggestions. He thought he was so proud of her. She also had Ivan's business cards printed which looked very dignified. They were gold emblazoned with raised capital black letters. She thought he would be pleased. She was going to meet him at Curly's again and give him everything.

Ivan was more than pleased with everything Donna gave him. His new cards had his name and his title as Property Manager on it and also had all of his contact numbers where he could be reached. He was so proud of it. He loved the raised bold black letters on his gold card. He gave one to Darlene, the waitress, right away. He thanked Donna again. He was going to do the best job for her ever. He had never had anyone believe in him like she did. He loved his job and the responsibilities that came with it. He was determined to make her proud.

Ivan stopped by Curly's early one morning on his way to the apartments. He went in and sat in the back booth where he usually sat.

> "Hi big guy. How have you been?"

> "Great, I'm hungry. How about a steak, eggs, hash browns, toast and a cup of hot chocolate?"

> "You got it." She said.

They weren't that busy and she came over to chat with him.

> "Darlene, would you like to go out with me sometime?"

> "Sure, when?"

> "When is your day off?"

"This Saturday I'm free."

"Me too. Do you like to bike ride?"

"I'm not sure. I've never tried it."

"Well there is always a first time. Why don't I pick you up at your place and you can try it?"

"Okay, I'm game."

"Let me have your address and phone number."

She wrote it down and gave it to him.

"I'll come and get you about 11:00. You don't have a helmet, do you?"

"Are you kidding? Of course not."

"Well, I'll bring one for you."

She said, "Do I have to wear it?"

Ivan said, "Well it's a lot safer. Any special color you'd like?"

"Surprise me."

"Okay." He said.

Ivan arrived at 11:00 on Saturday for Darlene.

"Hop on Darlene, try the helmet on."

It was bright pink.

"I like the color."

She struggled putting it on.

"My hair will never be the same," she said.

63

Ivan said, "Oh it will spring back up."

"Where are we going?"

"How about we drive down by the ocean? We can stop for lunch when we get hungry. Put your arms around my waist and your feet here. When we turn a corner, you kind of lean with me. Ready?"

"I think so."

She sounded a little shaky. VaVaVoom and they were off. Darlene gulped and hung onto Ivan for dear life. They rode for about an hour down the coast.

When they stopped at a light, Ivan said, "Darlene are you still back there?"

"I think so."

"If you're hungry we'll stop pretty soon. There's a good restaurant coming up."

Ivan pulled into the parking lot of the restaurant. He noticed Darlene was a little wobbly on her pins but she was anxious to get inside.

"I'll be back in a minute Ivan, I want to fix my hair."

She went to the ladies' room and felt nauseous. When she came out, she joined Ivan in a booth and they ordered cold drinks first.

Ivan said, "Now that wasn't so bad, was it? I think you did pretty good. We'll head back after lunch." Ivan ordered Darlene a small salad and a double cheeseburger for himself with fries. "I think this will be enough for the first time, Darlene."

When he dropped Darlene off at her place, she was still kind of shaky. "Maybe we can see a movie one night, Darlene?"

"That sounds good Ivan."

She started to give him her helmet.

"No, you keep it. It's a gift and pink isn't a good color on me anyway."

She laughed.

"Thank you, big guy."

Ivan met Donna at Curly's on Friday. It was payday and this was his first check that would reflect his pay increase as Donna's full-time property manager. They ordered their usual drinks. Coffee for her and hot chocolate with whipped cream for him. When he opened the envelope, she gave him he was elated. The check was over what he expected.

"Thank you, Donna."

"You deserve it Ivan."

"I'm going to open an account and bank this right away."

"Good idea, Ivan."

"What bank do you use?"

She told him and she gave him the manager's card there who was very helpful.

"This is a form to have your check "directly deposited" into your checking account if you wish

65

to open one. The manager is more than happy to help you, Ivan, with any questions, opening a checking or savings account, etc. He will take good care of you."

"Thank you, Donna."

"You can also stipulate a certain portion of your check to be automatically deposited in your savings account if you wish to open one."

"I like those ideas Donna."

"Well, they just help to make your life a little easier."

David could not believe how well the apartments were being managed without him. He had heard through the grapevine and could see for himself that Donna was doing a great job. She had surprised him. He couldn't get over it and this upset him to no end.

Leo was the only eviction at the apartments coming up. Donna thought she should go with Ivan since it was his first eviction. He was already two months behind in back rent, which wasn't unusual. Knocking on his door she said loudly,

"Open up Leo."

He finally opened the door and thrust an envelope at her.

"Here is all your back rent."

She was surprised and wondered how he came up with so much money especially in cash. Leo shut his door abruptly. She knocked on his door again. Leo barely re-opened it. "What is it this time?"

Donna said, "I hope this doesn't happen again, Leo."

He thought, I've had it with this bitch. No more! He despised Donna and loved causing her problems. She had called the police on hi m many times. He didn't say a word, and closed his door.

CHAPTER 10

The minute Donna and David's divorce was final Bill didn't waste any time and moved into Donna's home right away. Everything seemed to be going along fine. But she noticed the subject of marriage came up more and more frequently.

When Donna saw her father, she said, "Dad, Bill and I have become more serious and are thinking about marriage in the near future."

"Honey, you have to promise me something. This is very important."

"What is it Dad?"

"Please do not commingle your money with Bill's. Keep everything separate. Be sure to keep all your money and your assets in your name. Keep everything separate for at least six months."

"But he'll ask why," "What should I say?"

"Tell him you are in the process of a very complicated transaction and your lawyer and CPA have told you to do this until it is finalized. Do you understand?"

"Yes Dad, I'll do whatever you want."

"Promise me."

"Yes, I promise."

Nothing had changed with Bill in the sexual department. Donna was still more concerned with her mental state especially after her break-up with David. Before she knew it she and Bill were married. It wasn't long before Bill began to show his true colors after two and a half months of marriage. He always seemed to have a drink in his hand and a bottle close by. Bill ignored Donna unless it was to say something abusive to her and he liked to threaten her when he had been drinking all day. She knew he had a gun and became terrified of him. Donna's father was right about Bill. Don saw through Bill from the beginning. Donna knew something was wrong. One morning he didn't get up to go to work.

"Bill, aren't you going in to work today? You've had a lot of sick time lately."

"I'm not going in. In fact, I'm never going in."

"What do you mean Bill?"

"It means I've quit!"

"Why?"

"I need some time off for a while."

Donna said, "I see."

Donna was getting sick and tired of coming home and seeing him lying around doing nothing. Then she noticed that he started drinking excessively during the day and night. The last straw was he was not showering on a regular basis and looking very unkempt. She could always tell which room he was in by the odor.

She thought "I can't stand this any longer. I've got to do something. Dad was right."

Donna's father couldn't stand Bill and didn't want to be anywhere near him. Don would politely refuse any invitation from Donna if he knew Bill would be there. He didn't trust him, he always said that Bill had shifty eyes and would never look at you directly. Now that she thought about it Sheila and Bob weren't crazy about him either. Donna thought she should have introduced him to Murphy, her father's boxer, right from the beginning and maybe all this mess could have been avoided. Murphy and her father Don were excellent judges of people.

Donna couldn't believe how such an attractive and supposedly nice man could become such a monster in such a short time. But she thought it wasn't very smart of her to tell him everything about herself, especially her financial information, her privileged upbringing and affluent family, her net worth, her home in Palos Verdes, how many properties she owned, etc. and of course her marital problems with David. Bill was so clever and he knew just the right questions to ask at their sessions. The picture couldn't have been any clearer, but she just didn't see it. She needed someone she could talk to, a real professional who could help her. Boy could she pick 'em. Bill had even encouraged her about getting a divorce from David.

"Bill you really need some help,"

"You're all the help I need sweetheart."

And he resumed drinking and watching television. Donna walked out of the room. As she went outside, she grabbed her cell phone and called her attorney Irv Cohen and explained the situation to him. She made an appointment for the following day to start divorce proceedings. Then she called Ivan.

"Ivan, this is Donna. I need you right away at my house."

She explained the problem she was having with Bill to him.

"I'll be there in 15 minutes Donna."

"Thank you, Ivan."

In less than 15 minutes she heard the big Harley coming up the driveway. She told Ivan the divorce papers were in process and would be sent to Bill's attorney, Jack Barnes. She noticed Ivan always carried a gun. She was glad he had a license to carry.

"Ivan, threaten him all you want, but don't hurt him."

"Don't worry Donna this is what I do. I'll have him out of here pronto and believe me he won't be back."

Ivan entered the house, Donna pointed to the study.

"He's in there. Just follow the TV sounds."

"Stay here Donna."

Ivan saw Bill sprawled out on the sofa with a drink in his hand and a bottle on the coffee table. When Bill saw Ivan, he said, "Who the hell are you?"

> "I'm your worst enemy Bill. Donna wants you out of her house right now!! I'll give you 15 minutes. Take a bag with whatever you need for a few days and get the hell out of here. Donna will pack up all your things and have them sent to your attorney Jack Barnes. Jack also will have copies of the divorce papers for you. There will be no further communication of any kind between you and Donna. If I hear differently I can assure you no one will ever recognize you by your face again. Do you understand?"

Bill shakily got to his feet.

> "Now get going. You now have 10 minutes!"

Bill threw some personal things in a bag and got into his car. He left as fast as he could. Ivan was glad that Bill was out of Donna's life. He was one mean hombre and not to be trusted. Ivan vowed if Bill bothered Donna one more time he would get rid of him permanently. His biker brothers understood situations like this and they would help him dispose of Bill without a trace.

The next day Donna met Irv at his office and they covered all the details of the divorce. He told her he would send a copy to her right away and Fed-Ex a copy to Bill's attorney. He felt sure he would be able to have their marriage annulled since they were only married a couple of months.

"Donna there is something else I would like you to do."

"What is that Irv?"

"I'm concerned about your safety. I would like you to sign a restraining order right now against Bill, and I will include the restraining order with the divorce papers I'll be sending to Bill's lawyer. That way if he violates it and approaches you he can be legally locked up for a while."

"That sounds like a good idea. Let's do it Irv."

Irv said "The thought of being in jail just might discourage him from bothering you anymore."

After the fiasco with Bill, Donna needed to get away. She called her Dad and they went to one of their favorite spots for dinner.

"Dad I really need to get away for a couple of days. I'll be leaving for Catalina tomorrow."

"Honey I don't know why you like to go there especially by yourself."

"Dad, that's the whole point. You know how much I enjoy the people there and all that shopping. I'll call you the minute I get home."

Before she left for Catalina Donna had her security service stop by and change all the house locks and install a better security system.

Don suddenly thought of something he could do for his daughter while she was in Catalina. His mind was going a mile a minute. This might be just the perfect time to find her another townhouse as nice, or even better than her last one. Maybe even with an ocean view. He and Murphy, would scout the area. He knew there was a new townhouse development in the area. It looked like it was almost finished. Murphy loved going with Don in the car and vice versa. Don thought the sooner she was out of that big house the better. Too many bad memories. He wanted her to feel like herself again.

The next day Don saw they had put up the for-sale signs on the new development that was near his estate in Palos Verdes. Don liked that it was a gated community, which he wanted for his daughter. He stopped and went in the real estate office on the site. The realtor was very pleasant and showed him a complete work-up they had of all the floor plans. Most of the townhouses had ocean views and Don asked the realtor when he might see some of the models. She said in about a week. He said that would be perfect and she said she would call him when the models were ready to view. Don could hardly wait.

Bill made an appointment with his attorney, Jack Barnes. He was anxious to see his part of the divorce settlement. Jack asked him to come into his office and Bill took a seat across from Jack and could barely contain himself.

Jack said, "These are for you Bill."

He handed him a copy of the divorce papers and also the restraining order filed against him by Donna. Bill took the papers and stuffed them in his jacket pocket.

> "I am curious Jack, what will my part of the settlement be?"

> "Well Bill, I'm afraid you are not entitled to any settlement."

Bill sat there stunned.

> "What? That can't be, Jack! What do you mean?"

> "It simply means that you and Donna did not co-mingle any of your monies and assets."

There was a long silence. Bill just sat there fuming. "That bitch!" He thought.

Bill said, "Can't we contest this?"

> "No, Bill, I'm afraid we can't."

He remembered Donna had said something about keeping all their assets separate for six months and he had forgotten all about it.

> "Also, Bill, you and Donna were only married for two and a half months. Her attorney is also in the process of having the marriage annulled. As a reminder, Bill, Donna has a restraining order filed against you for her protection. I gave you a copy of that with your divorce papers."

Fuming, Bill got up to leave.

Jack said, "Bill don't forget to take the box of your belongings that Donna sent here. They are by my secretary, Alice's desk."

When Bill was gone, Jack said to Alice,

> "I hope we don't see him again. I wish I had never taken him on as a client."

Bill was seething walking to his car in the building's garage. He thought

> "I'll track that bitch down and make her pay for all of this."

CHAPTER 11

The months had dragged by since David had left Sandy. She was still depressed and very lonely. She couldn't get David out of her mind. She missed him so much. She had found out where he and his wife lived and thought maybe she would just drive by. As she drove by she noticed that there were no cars in the driveway. She decided to park the car down the street and walk up the steep side of the house out of curiosity. She noticed that one side was covered by tall green vegetation which would provide a good cover for her. There had been some rain recently off and on but she had on her durable hiking boots and was not worried if they got wet. As Sandy neared the top of the steep grade she saw the warning signs that were set up. Danger, Private Property, No Trespassing. There was a huge pile of construction material lying on the ground and half of the barricade had been removed. They were obviously planning on putting in some kind of retaining wall for security and safety, but had to temporarily postpone their work because of the rainy weather. Sandy stood by the opening looking down into the ravine below. She realized she was dangerously close to the edge of a steep cliff which dropped straight down to a rocky ravine. It was a sunny day and Sandy's long blonde hair shone through the vegetation. Sandy did not realize she was not alone.

77

Someone was watching her and thought, "What in the hell is Donna doing out here?"

It looked like she was in some kind of trance.

Sandy was actually thinking, "What am I doing here? I must be crazy."

Unfortunately, those were Sandy's last thoughts. A hand suddenly shot out and slammed into her back with a violent push. She went tumbling down the steep cliff landing in the deep ravine below.

Two teenage boys had been hiking and were looking through their binoculars in the area when they spotted the body in the ravine shortly afterwards. Their parents called 911 immediately. Patrol officers were immediately dispatched to the scene at the top of the cliff on the Collins' property. Officers cordoned off the area to preserve the crime scene, and called in the crime scene and forensics units. When that was complete they sent a special recovery team to go down in the ravine to bring the body up to the top. The team was experienced in climbing down areas that could be treacherous and slippery.

Donna came home from Catalina to discover that she was not allowed access into her home unless she showed some identification.

Donna's reaction was, "Oh my God. I knew something like this would happen."

It was a painstaking process but they were able to recover the body faster than they thought. When they reached the top of the cliff with the body on the stretcher it was placed in the coroner's van and immediately taken to the medical examiner's office.

Donna spent a quiet evening at home. She felt sorry for whoever fell down the cliff. She couldn't figure out why anyone would be up there in the first place. But in her mind, she kept blaming David over and over for what had happened. He should have put in that wall the very first thing. When he finally decided to, they had bad weather for a few months with rains off and on and the wall had to be postponed. Now it was too late, things happen. The weather was finally starting to turn nice again and she would have it done immediately, sell the damn place and get the hell out of there.

Still fuming after his visit with his attorney, Bill left California for his hometown of Portland, Oregon immediately. He tossed his cell phone in a dumpster and bought a cheap burner phone. He drove straight through and did not tell anyone he had left California. When he arrived in Portland he found an inexpensive apartment right away that had a parking space available for his car. The next day he went to the public library to look at recent casualties and obituaries in the Southern California newspapers. He didn't find what he was looking for but he would check the next day.

CHAPTER 12

Lieutenant Stephen McClary worked for the Los Angeles Police Department (LAPD) and was in charge of the homicide division. He was a very dignified looking man in his forties tall and very attractive. He had been in the position of lieutenant for about ten years and loved it. Lieutenant McClary's wife had passed away about five years ago. They never had any children. They had been happily married for fifteen years and he missed her terribly. She had become sick with a terminal illness and had passed away suddenly. He was devastated when he lost her. He always said, "Thank God for my work." He threw himself into it relentlessly and tried not to think of anything else. It didn't occur to him to date or find anyone else. He tried to fulfill the emptiness in his life by being the best in his field and he was. The lieutenant was a "hands on" type of lieutenant. He liked to be involved and know what cases his detectives were working on and what progress was being made. If there were any problems they knew he was always there for them. He would always stand behind them and wasn't one to tolerate high JINGO, LAPD jargon for office politics. His staff respected him and they did their best for him. The lieutenant's detective teams were always at the very top for closed cases.

Lieutenant McClary called his top two-man detective
team into his office, Ramon Ruiz and his partner Ted
Sicilliano. Ramon was the lead detective and without a
doubt the best detective the lieutenant had ever worked
with. He was also the best looking detective in the office.
Ramon spoke Spanish fluently if needed which had come
in handy more times than the lieutenant could recall.
Ramon and Ted worked well together and he considered
them his very best detective team. Ramon and Ted were
also very good friends. Ramon was single and his Latino
good looks made him a babe magnet. No wonder the
young women in the office were always flirting with him.
Ted and his wife, Janet had been happily married for ten
years. They were a close knit Italian family and had two
small children. They were always trying to fix Ramon up
with a blind date. Ramon had put his foot down after the
last one.

"No more, guys."

And that was the end of that.

The detectives came into his office and sat down across
from him. The lieutenant said, "We have a new homicide
case. The victim, a woman, was spotted by two teenage
boys with binoculars at the bottom of a deep ravine in
Palos Verdes. It was determined she fell from the top of
the cliff located on the property of Mr. and Mrs. David
Collins in Palos Verdes. Forensics has concluded she was
not alone from the two different shoe impressions left at
the top of the cliff. The impressions were not crystal clear
because of the weather conditions, but fairly accurate.
The one set of impressions was a size 11 and the other
was the victims."

At first, the lieutenant was concerned about extracting the body safely from the ravine. He had called in a special crime scene team that specialized in treacherous and rocky areas. He told them if they felt it was unsafe for them he would call in a helicopter and could lower a stretcher and drop lines down to them at the bottom of the ravine and they could bring her up that way. The team assured him they could do it safely without the helicopter but appreciated it. The weather had turned pleasant and now appeared to be on the sunny side. Slippage was no longer a problem for them either as the sun was drying everything out. They were able to bring the victim up safely on a stretcher to the top of the cliff.

They said the time of death was between three and four in the afternoon. Facial and body injuries were caused by the fall. The victim did not have an ID on her, but her car keys were still in her pocket.

The lieutenant said to Ramon, "You will probably find the car close by in the area. Take the evidence bag with her car keys and see if you can find it. There is probably a driver's license in the glove compartment and maybe a cell phone. Get back to me right away on your progress. Also, I'll put more officers in the area to check house to house again to see if we can find some witnesses or somebody that has some useful information. Thank you, Ramon and Ted."

"We're on it, lieutenant."

CHAPTER 13

Dr. Josh Ryan, the medical examiner knew they were bringing in a woman victim soon. He had heard the news about a woman who had fallen off a steep cliff in Palos Verdes into a ravine below. The cause of the accident had not been released yet. They brought Sandy into the room and placed her on the table in the autopsy room. Josh always tried to remain impassive and focus on his work, but sometimes it was difficult, and this was one of those times. He couldn't imagine what this young woman had just gone through. He could tell she must have been very beautiful. She didn't need this to happen in the prime of her life. Surprisingly, her color still looked fairly good. He didn't know why but he touched the side of her neck. He stopped suddenly. He thought he felt something. He placed his hand on her neck again. And he couldn't believe it. There was a faint PULSE!!! GOOD GRIEF, SHE WAS STILL ALIVE, BUT BARELY!! Josh hit the PA system in his building.

He loudly cried, "EMERGENCY TEAM TO THE AUTOPSY ROOM!! NOW!! ON THE DOUBLE!!"

His team came rushing through the door in seconds.

"THIS VICTIM IS ALIVE, BUT JUST BARELY! Attach all life support equipment and get her hooked up to an IV immediately!!! The minute she's

83

ready to go put her on the stretcher and rush her to ER at USC Medical Center."

Each team member knew exactly what to do. Josh had trained them for this very thing even though no one had ever expected it to happen. But it did, and they were ready.

Josh said to one of his aides, Jim, "Alert Bob, to bring the ambulance around. We are bringing her out now. I want you to go with her in the ambulance Jim. Call me when she is in the ER and let me know her status before you return. I'm calling the director now at SC to let him know what's happening. I'll tell him you'll be there as fast as you can."

Josh could see his team had done a number one job on Sandy. He called the director on his emergency speed dial at SC. The director picked up immediately when he saw his emergency phone ring.

"Robert, this is Josh."

He told him what was happening and that the ambulance should be there shortly.

"I'll alert everyone here Josh."

"Thank you Robert. Maybe she'll have a second chance."

"Let's hope so." They both said.

Josh called his lieutenant friend Stephen McClary at his office to let him know what had happened. Stephen was at a loss for words. "Let's pray that she makes it Josh. This is unbelievable. I am going to call the D.A. right now. I want to keep this quiet for her safety and recovery. Can you keep this under wraps temporarily?"

"You bet Stephen. Whatever it takes."

CHAPTER 14

After talking to Josh, the Lieutenant called the District Attorney, Elliot Harper, to apprise him of the unusual situation. He would rather do it in person rather than a phone call. He would ask him if he was available for an early dinner as soon as possible. The situation was too complicated to discuss on the phone. He had Elliot's direct line and he picked up right away when he saw who was calling.

"Hi Stephen, good to hear from you. What's up? Anything I need to know?"

"I'm glad I caught you in."

"You're not going to believe what I have to tell you, Elliot. It's an urgent matter that you need to know about now. I'd rather not discuss it on the phone. Can you meet me for an early dinner tonight? I'll treat, you pick the place and make it a good one. And believe me, you will need a good strong drink or two when you hear what I have to tell you."

"You're on. I'm very curious, Stephen. It sounds urgent."

"It is."

85

"How about Melvin's at 6:00? I'll make the reservation at my private table."

"Sounds good Elliot, see you there."

When Stephen arrived at Melvin's he asked the maitre'd to take him to Elliott Harper's table. When Stephen was seated he said,

"Let's order a drink right away. I need one and you will too, this is unbelievable."

The waiter came and took their order for two vodka martinis with olives. Stephen told the story about Sandy's fall from the beginning to the end. The medical examiner, Josh, called him when Sandy was brought in the autopsy room and he told him Sandy was still alive. Just barely but she was still alive. They rushed her immediately to SC and they are currently working on her in the ER. Elliott sat there not moving,

"What an amazing story Stephen."

"I would like to keep this under wraps for the time being, Elliott, for two reasons. First, we are getting too close to nailing a suspect now and I don't want to put her in any danger or jeopardy. And second, I don't want the media sticking their nose in this. She is lucky enough to survive this."

"I couldn't agree with you more Stephen."

"When do you want to go public with this?"

"When we catch the suspect and she is able to leave the hospital."

"Who knows about this Stephen?"

"Myself, Josh, you and the doctors taking care of her."

"I'm behind you 100% on this Stephen."

The waiter came by again to see if they had decided on what they would like for dinner. They were both so caught up by all of this that they had completely forgotten about eating. Stephen said,

"Let's order, Elliott, and I could use another drink. How about you?"

They ordered the house special, dover sole for both of them and another drink.

CHAPTER 15

Donna's phone rang early one morning.

"Hello Mrs. Collins, this is Lieutenant Steven McClary from the LAPD, the Los Angeles Police Department."

"Lieutenant how can I help you?"

"It's in regard to the fall of a woman recently on your property down to the ravine below."

"I see."

"Would it be possible to see you for a few minutes this morning? I just have a few routine questions."

"Of course."

"10:00 o'clock would be fine."

When the lieutenant came to the door Donna was impressed. He looked like he was in his early forties, tall, about 6′3″ with thick black hair with a few gray specks. Very dignified looking. He gave her his card.

"Come in lieutenant. I just made some fresh coffee. Would you like some?"

"No thank you Mrs. Collins."

"When you called, I thought I heard you say you were in the police department, but I see from your card that you are specifically in charge of the homicide division."

"Yes, that is correct."

"Is there some reason to think this may not have been an accident?"

"We're just trying to cover all the bases at this time."

"Well I don't know if I can help you. I can't think of anything that might be helpful."

"Mrs. Collins, just for the record can you tell me where you were yesterday between three and four o'clock in the afternoon?"

"Yes, I was in Catalina. Lieutenant, am I a suspect?"

"No, not at all. These are just routine questions. Is your husband, Mr. Collins home now?"

"No lieutenant, we are divorced. I have his cell number if you need to reach him."

"Yes, thank you Mrs. Collins. If you hear from him, please tell him that I need to talk to him right away."

"I will. Also, lieutenant you should know I remarried on "the rebound" as they say, which was very unfortunate, to a Dr. Bill Townsend. My attorney is in the process of having the marriage

89

annulled since we were married such a short time and has also put out a restraining order against him. I guess it was a good thing I had not changed my last name from the first marriage."

The lieutenant said, "I am sorry to hear about that Mrs. Collins. I gather you have apparently had serious problems with Dr. Townsend?"

"Yes, shortly after we were married, he turned into a Jekyll and Hyde personality, quit his job, refused to work and became an alcoholic. He became violent and I am afraid of him. I know he has a gun and he has threatened me with it. He was left nothing in the divorce settlement and is quite angry and bitter about it. I guess he thought he would make quite a bit from the settlement."

"Do you have an address or phone number where I can reach him?"

"No, I'm sorry lieutenant, but I can give you his attorney's name and number if that will help."

"Do you know if he has any living relatives?"

"No Lieutenant. His father was the only one and he passed away from natural causes before we were married."

"Thank you, Mrs. Collins. You've been very helpful."

"If anything comes up later that might be helpful, Mrs. Collins, please give me a call at any time. All of my phone numbers are on the card, including my home as well. Thank you for seeing me today."

"You're welcome."

The lieutenant thought she was very polite and very pretty. There was something about her deep blue eyes that fascinated him.

CHAPTER 16

Ramon and Ted searched the area thoroughly for a car that looked out of place by the Collins residence. The found a little Toyota Corolla and tried the key from the evidence bag. It was the victim's car. They found her driver's license in the glove compartment and also a cell phone. They saw the driver's license listed a P.O. Box number for her address. They could check with the post office to see if she had an actual home address and also any mail which had not been picked up. Maybe something would turn up that would be helpful about her personal life. Ramon also saw a decal on the inside window of the driver's side which identified a boat owner's decal for restricted parking and what marina the boat was in. He told Ted they could check the Department of Marine Services for the specific marina and then contact that marina for the gangway and slip number. Ramon called the lieutenant with the good news.

"Good work guys."

Ramon said, "Lieutenant the victim's name is Sandy Grant."

"Have copies made of her picture from her driver's license, Ramon. That should help a lot in your investigation. Come to my office Ramon when you have the pictures and we'll make an appointment with Mrs. Collins to see if she recognizes her. Then we will do the same with her ex-husbands, Mr. Collins and Dr. Bill Townsend."

Ramon had the victim's picture blown up and came to the lieutenant's office and showed him the pictures.

The lieutenant said, "HOLY SHIT!! SHE LOOKS JUST LIKE MRS. COLLINS! THEY LOOK ENOUGH ALIKE TO BE TWINS!! I CAN'T BELIEVE THIS!! You know Ramon, it's been said that we all have a look alike somewhere. I think I'm becoming a believer, maybe Mrs. Collins can lend some insight into this when we talk with her."

Ramon and Ted continued their investigation. He called the lieutenant right away when he and Ted located Sandy's boat in the San Pedro marina.

"Lieutenant the boat is her primary residence. It's called "Sandy's Getaway" and is on gangway 15, slip 4. We'll get a search warrant going right away."

The lieutenant said, "Good work guys."

"Ted and I are going to start canvassing the area now and see if anyone recognizes her picture. We have a good feeling about this lieutenant."

"Go for it guys."

Ramon and Ted headed towards a bar and restaurant called "The Wharf". It was within walking distance of Sandy's boat.

As soon as Ramon and Ted had the search warrant they started going through Sandy's boat looking for any clues which might have been missed after forensics completed their investigation. Ramon found a box of letters that Sandy had saved. He called the lieutenant.

> "Lieutenant, Sandy has a box of letters which might be helpful. It looks like she was close to someone in the Northern California area, the return address is all the same. I will go through them in the evening when I get home and see what I can determine. There are quite a few letters over a long period of time. I'll get back to you as soon as I have something."

> "Okay Ramon, maybe this will help us."

Ramon set aside so many hours each night when he came home from work to read Sandy's letters. There were quite a few. She had had a difficult youth going from foster home to foster home in here early years. When she reached sixteen the foster home she was in had to give her up because of financial trouble. She had been going to a nearby school for her education and had become best friends with a girl named Alecia who was her own age. Alecia and her family grew to love Sandy and considered her part of their family. When she told them she had to leave and go to another foster home the father told her to pack her things and wait for them outside and they

would pick her up in fifteen minutes. Do not tell anyone.
They rescued her and took her into their family
permanently.

Sandy apparently excelled in her studies at school and
eventually took business classes at a junior college for two
years and then completed two more years at the
university where she lived. She took a lot of night classes
and worked part-time as a secretary to help pay for her
schooling. She got a BA degree in business at night
school and also online classes. She fell in love with a
salesman at her part-time job and they were happily
married for five years and then moved to Southern
California in Marina del Rey. He had gotten a better job
opportunity there and they both had always wanted to
live by the ocean. The girls kept up their close friendship
and wrote to each other a few times each year. They were
really like sisters. Alecia and her husband had one son,
Brian.

Ramon related the story to the lieutenant. Sandy had
such a tumultuous childhood in the foster homes and
then a sad ending to her marriage three years after they
moved to Marina del Rey her husband was killed in a car
accident. After reading all the letters Ramon was so
saddened by the turn of events in Sandy's life. And now
this, pushed down that steep cliff. Sometimes life was so
unfair. He told the lieutenant everything he had learned.

> "Do you want me to notify the family she used to
> live with?"

95

"Not just yet, Ramon. I'll tell you why soon. I'm waiting for some additional information."

"Okay lieutenant. Let me know."

CHAPTER 17

David had an urgent message on his phone to call a Lieutenant McClary at the (LAPD) Los Angeles Police Department. He didn't know what it was about but thought it was best to find out right away. He dialed the lieutenant's direct number that he had given him on his cell phone.

"Lieutenant McClary speaking."

"Hello lieutenant, this is David Collins returning your call. You left a message for me to call you. "What is it about?"

"Mr. Collins, do you have time to stop by our station today? I have a few questions to ask you about a woman who fell into the ravine by your house."

David said "I can be at your station in about a half an hour. Is that okay?"

"Yes, see you then."

When David arrived, the lieutenant said, "Let's go into my office Mr. Collins. It's a little quieter in there. Can I get you some coffee or something to drink?"

"No thank you, I'm okay."

"Mr. Collins I would like to show you a picture of the woman who fell into the ravine by your house. Does she look familiar to you, or do you recognize her?"

The lieutenant instantly saw the look of recognition and shock on David's face.

"Everyone says it is best to call your attorney before answering any questions, lieutenant."

"That's your prerogative Mr. Collins. We are just gathering information right now. By the way, can you tell me where you were yesterday between three and four in the afternoon when this happened?"

"Not really. I am a real estate investor in apartment buildings and I was out looking for properties that are undervalued to purchase."

"I see said the lieutenant. If you can think of anyone you may have talked to or someone that saw you during that time-frame please call me. Here is my card with all my numbers. Feel free to call me at any time. I'll walk you out Mr. Collins. Please don't leave the area in case we have more questions. Thank you, Mr. Collins."

When David got back in his truck he couldn't believe how drastically his life had changed overnight. He had made a bad mistake picking Sandy to have sex with and it turned out to be a whopper. It had cost him dearly. His marriage was over and many of the properties he worked so hard on were given to Donna in the divorce settlement. It had become a bitter pill for him to swallow. Why did women always make such a big deal out of these things? It was fun while it lasted but that was all it was. They took these things too seriously. He always remembered Donna's father Don saying more than once that "Donna's pencil has no eraser". Donna had her pick of the properties in the settlement as well as the house. She naturally chose the apartments with the most upside. This whole thing annoyed him to no end.

CHAPTER 18

The lieutenant called Ramon and Ted into his office. The lieutenant said, "David Collins and Dr. Bill Townsend are persons of interest in the Sandy Grant case. I don't see Donna Collins as a person of interest or suspect unless she hired someone to murder Sandy. She was in Catalina and on the Catalina Express coming back at the time. In addition to pictures of Sandy, also have pictures of David Collins and Dr. Bill Townsend blown up for your investigation. Keep trying to reach Dr. Townsend and bring him in for questioning."

The following day the lieutenant called Ramon in his office again. When Ramon sat down across from the lieutenant he saw the serious look on his face.

> "Ramon, I want you and Ted to make Sandy Grant's case your number one priority. I'm getting a lot of pressure from up above because of the influential neighborhood where this occurred. Maybe the pictures we have of the victim, Sandy, David Collins and Dr. Townsend will help you and Ted come up with something. Get back to me right away on your progress. Thank you, guys."

> "We're on it lieutenant."

CHAPTER 19

"Hello Mrs. Collins, this is lieutenant McClary again. Something has come up that you may be able to help us with. Do you have a few minutes now? We are in the neighborhood."

"Yes, that will be all right."

When Lieutenant McClary and Ramon arrived, Donna met them at the door.

"Come in please."

The lieutenant introduced her to Ramon.

"Can I get you anything? Coffee perhaps, or a cold drink?"

"No thank you. We're okay. Mrs. Collins, I'd like to show you a picture of someone. Do you recognize this woman, or does she look familiar to you?"

Donna froze when she saw the picture.

"Lieutenant, this looks exactly like the woman my husband was having an affair with. I hate to say it, but we do look a lot like each other."

"Yes, you do."

"Is this the woman they found in the ravine?"

"Yes, it is."

"Oh."

"Mrs. Collins, have you seen or talked to either of your ex-husbands recently?"

"No, not since we divorced."

"Thank you, Mrs. Collins. If you speak to either one please have them call me at once. I'll try calling them again."

"Mrs. Collins, how did you know what the woman looked like?"

"I found photos of her in my husband's truck by accident."

"I see." said the lieutenant. "Mrs. Collins, do you know the shoe size of your husbands?"

"I believe David is a size 11, I'm not sure about Bill."

The lieutenant thanked her for her help as they left her home.

"You're welcome Lieutenant."

"Feel free to call me anytime, Mrs. Collins, if you think of anything else."

"Thank you, lieutenant."

When they left Donna was thinking, "I wonder if David or Bill did kill her. Bill might have thought it was me. David had motive enough to kill either me or that other woman."

When they returned to their car the lieutenant said, "Ramon, let's hope the pictures of the victim, David Collins, and Dr. Townsend help when canvassing."

"Yes sir."

The lieutenant said, "David certainly had enough motive and opportunity to kill Mrs. Collins or Sandy, and Bill could have mistaken Sandy for Donna. He also had enough motive and opportunity. I think they both got quite a jolt when their part of the divorce settlement was explained."

Ramon said, "We still have been unable to locate Bill at his address and he has left no forwarding address. We also checked with Bill's attorney and he has no idea where he is."

The lieutenant said "Maybe he went back to the area where he is from in Portland, Oregon. Start checking for him there. We may end up having to send you guys up there."

CHAPTER 20

Ramon and Ted started to canvass the area by Sandy's boat, they went into "The Wharf" and showed their badges to the bartender, Charlie.

"Charlie, we have a couple of pictures we would like you to look at."

Ramon showed him Sandy's picture first.

"Do you recognize her?"

"I sure do!" he said. "A real looker. She comes in frequently."

"Does she come in by herself or with someone?"

"By herself usually."

"Does she talk to anyone or seem friendly to anyone in particular?"

"Now that you mention it, she has been talking to a good-looking guy at the bar."

"What does he look like?" "Pretty tall, about 6'3". Good looking guy. I hadn't seen him in here before."

Ramon showed him David's picture. "Is this the guy?"

"Yeah it is."

"Does this guy look familiar?"

He showed Charlie a picture of Dr. Townsend.

"No, I've never seen him before." Charlie said, "I hope Sandy is okay. She's a very nice person."

"Thank you for your help Charlie."

Ramon laid a twenty on the counter for him as he and Ted left.

CHAPTER 21

The lieutenant called Mr. Collins on his cell phone. David answered,

"Hello."

"Mr. Collins, this is Lieutenant McClary. Could you stop by my office again? I know we spoke before but I have some more information for you."

"Yes lieutenant. I'm about ten minutes away. Is now a good time?"

"Yes, it is."

David came in and sat across from the lieutenant.

"I know you wished to talk to your lawyer before David, however, if you cooperate with us we might be able to help you more. Is it alright if I call you David?"

"Yes. What information do you have lieutenant?"

"Well we know you met the victim, Sandy Grant at The Wharf. We have evidence that you have been on her boat and it appears you were having an affair with her."

"Yes, lieutenant, I fixed some things for her on her boat and things got a little out of hand. When she gave me some nude photos of her I ended the relationship, but I didn't kill her lieutenant. I swear."

The lieutenant thought David looked sad and remorseful and he thought he was being truthful, but sometimes they could fool you. The lieutenant said to David we have not been able to locate any family for Sandy. The Lieutenant thought that so long as David was there he would like to check his reaction to a few things.

"If you are interested, any burial expenses will be handled here, David sat there not saying a word. The lieutenant thought, well there is certainly no remorse here.

It was obvious that David had no interest or intention of contributing to any of her burial expenses. The lieutenant thought, I am beginning to dislike this guy more and more.

If David was grieving at all it was probably about his failed marriage and divorce settlement which had reduced his net worth substantially.

"We have no further questions for you at this time David, but please do not leave town for any reason."

"Yes lieutenant."

"If you think of anything else that might be helpful please do not hesitate to call me."

"Yes sir."

The lieutenant called Ramon into his office.

> "Ramon, Mr. Collins has now gone from a person
> of interest to a suspect. His affair with Sandy
> Grant is motive enough because she caused the
> break-up of his marriage, but we need to have
> more evidence to arrest him. There is also the
> possibility that he may have thought Sandy was
> his wife, Donna, and thought he would push her
> over the cliff to make it look like an accident. He
> has lost a lot of money in his divorce settlement
> and he is probably very bitter about it."

CHAPTER 22

The lieutenant talked to Ramon and Ted.

"You guys are doing good work and are making great progress. Also, I need you to dig deeper into the tenants at Donna's apartments. See if anyone stands out or is in any trouble of any kind. Get back to me as soon as you can. Thank you, guys. Keep it up."

Ramon knocked on the lieutenant's door.

"Come in Ramon."

"Lieutenant we think there is one tenant in Donna's apartment that stands out more than the others."

"Who is that Ramon?"

"A Leo Garcia. He was behind in his rent for two months and was going to be evicted. He somehow came up with the full two months back rent and gave it to Donna. He hasn't been working lately, not even anything temporary and when questioned he can't recall how he got that much money. I

109

think we should bring him in for further questioning."

"Do it right away and let me know when he is here. We will question him together."

Lieutenant McClary calls in his staff for a weekly update on the unsolved and solved homicides.

"I'm going to start today with the Sandy Grant case. We are making good progress and I want to update all of you. The wife, Mrs. Collins, is not a person of interest. She has a solid alibi. Her ex-husbands, however, have become suspects. David Collins has no alibi and he and Sandy Grant were having an affair. Forensics is going through Sandy's boat as we speak for more evidence. Mrs. Collins identified Sandy as the woman her husband was having the affair with. She found nude photos of Sandy in her husband's truck by accident. We have been unable to locate Dr. Bill Townsend who was briefly married to Mrs. Collins after her divorce from Mr. Collins. Dr. Townsend has become a suspect in the Sandy Grant case also. He may have thought that Sandy was Donna. They looked so much alike. Ramon and Ted are also checking the tenants again in Donna's apartments to see if anyone stands out as a problem or seems suspicious. There is one tenant, a Leo Garcia that stands out and we are bringing him in for further questioning. He was going to be evicted, but came up suddenly with cash to pay his two months back rent and doesn't recall what he did to earn the money. He has no job, permanent or temporary. I will continue to have weekly updates for all of you. I will update you tomorrow morning on the other outstanding crimes. Thank you."

CHAPTER 23

Ramon and Ted knock on Leo's door. Leo opens the door,

"What is it?"

"Hello Leo this is Ramon, again, and my partner Ted Sicilliano. We would like you to come down to the station with us. We have a few more questions."

Leo reluctantly goes with them in their car. The lieutenant comes into the interrogation room after they arrive.

"Hello Leo." the lieutenant said.

"Can we get you anything to drink?"

"A soda will be fine."

The lieutenant nodded to Ted and he went to get a soda. The lieutenant sat across from Leo.

"Leo, we are concerned that you can't recall how you came up with the two months back rent so suddenly. As I told you before, any information you can give us might help you considerably. Otherwise, I have to say this is looking highly suspicious. I have to be honest with you, Leo, this

112

is not looking good for you. Leo, did someone give you this much cash for a specific reason?"

"What do you mean, lieutenant, when you say any information I give you might help me?"

"Leo, we may have to hold you in jail until we clear this up. If you receive a sentence, we may be able to reduce your time in a maximum-security cell."

Leo knew what a maximum-security cell was like, but he felt that they didn't have enough evidence to hold him at this time and the lieutenant knew it too. Leo was quiet and finally said,

"I'm sorry lieutenant; I just can't remember how I had that much money."

"I think you are holding out on me Leo."

"No, I swear I'm not lieutenant."

He nodded to Ramon.

"We'll release you for now. Leo, but please don't leave the area."

Leo said "I think I need to talk to my attorney before I answer any more of your questions."

CHAPTER 24

Ramon and Ted were in the lieutenant's office.

Ramon said, "It looks like Dr. Townsend has left town. There is no forwarding address."

The lieutenant sat there thinking that maybe he had returned to where he used to live in Portland.

"I want you both to fly to Portland immediately and see if you can locate him there. Keep in touch with me on a daily basis. We'll get this nut eventually. I'll say this for him, he certainly picked the right occupation for himself."

Ramon and Ted flew to Portland and checked into an inexpensive but clean motel close to a diner. They came up blank with finding an address or a telephone number for Bill. They knew that if Bill was employed somewhere it had to be an affluent area because he liked to prey on wealthy women. They decided to check the mental health clinics and also hospitals in the most well to do areas of Portland to see if he was employed there. After many calls they finally located a small mental health clinic that employed a Dr. Bill Townsend in one of Portland's more affluent areas. The clinic said that Dr. Townsend had taken a few days off for personal business and would be back soon. Ramon and Ted went to the clinic and showed them their badges and asked to see the director, Mr. Burns. The director came out immediately. They introduced themselves and Ramon said, "Mr. Burns, we are trying to locate Dr. Townsend. We need to ask him some questions for a case we are working on in California."

The director was pleased to help them and gave them his address and phone number.

> "If you should hear from him, please call us immediately. We appreciate you keeping our meeting confidential."

> "Of course, detectives."

Ramon and Ted went through the procedure of getting a search warrant as quickly as possible in Portland to search Bill's apartment. They called the lieutenant to keep him apprised of what was happening. The lieutenant was delighted.

> "Keep it up guys. Let me know what you find in his apartment."

As soon as they had the search warrant they went to his apartment street address. They knocked on the manager's door, showed their badges and identified themselves.

> "We need to contact Dr. Townsend on a case we are working on in California. We need to have you

take us to his apartment, but first we would like to see if his car is here."

The manager said, "Let's check his space."

The car was there. Ramon felt the hood to see how it felt and it was cold. Bill was either in his apartment or he was in the wind. The manager knocked on Bill's door. No answer. "Bill, this is the manager. We need to check an electrical problem in your apartment. Please open the door."

Ramon and Ted had drawn their guns and asked the manager to stand back. Ramon took the master key from the manager and opened the door. He produced the search warrant for the manager before entering. Bill had gone somewhere.

> "We need about an hour to check everything. We will let you know when we are done. If you should hear from Bill, please let us know and we appreciate you keeping this confidential between us. Thank you."

They called the phone company to get a record of his calls for the last few days. When they had read his call log, they saw that he had called the airport in Portland recently. Ramon and Ted headed to the airport and checked the airlines that were going to California over the last few days. There was only one airline that showed a one-way flight booked to California. It was for a Paul Townsend that morning. Ramon and Ted showed the blown-up picture they had of Bill to the airlines, but there was no sign of recognition. They also looked through the security camera footage for any signs of him. Nothing there either. They called the lieutenant again. "It's a long shot lieutenant, but the name Paul Townsend sounds suspicious and might prove to be promising. We have a suggestion."

"Let me hear it."

"Why don't we come back to California and do some calling to the cheap motels in the San Pedro area and see if a Paul Townsend is staying there. It's a long shot, but if he is, we can go to the motel and see if the staff recognizes the picture we have of Bill."

"I like it. Go for it."

"We'll see you soon lieutenant. We'll get the first flight out."

Bill found what he was looking for in the California newspapers the second day after his return to Portland. An unidentified woman had fallen off a steep cliff into a ravine in the Palo Verdes area. An unidentified woman?? What in the hell happened?? Who in the hell is this unidentified woman?!?! Shook up, he dropped the newspaper on the floor. When he reached down to pick it up Donna's smiling face was looking up at him at one of her charity events. What the hell happened? He re-checked the newspaper date. It was today's date. The paper said the case was under investigation. He would keep checking the paper each day to see if they finally identified the woman. On the third day there was a small article saying the women's name was Sandy Grant. He turned to the obituaries and saw her picture. "SHIT."

He saw the resemblance to Donna immediately. Seething all the way back to his apartment, he grabbed the phone the minute he walked in and booked a flight to California early the next morning. He said out loud, "I won't fail this time Donna!"

He decided that he would rent a car while he was there with dark tinted windows. He didn't want anyone to recognize him in California. He made a reservation at an inexpensive motel he was familiar with in San Pedro and told them. "I am expecting a package from FedEx in a day or two. Please hold it for me." Since he was flying, he thought a gun might be necessary and come in handy. He put his gun in a package and went to FedEx and had it sent to the motel in California. He called the clinic where he worked in Portland early that morning and left a message. He had some urgent personal business to take care of and told them that he would be back in a few days.

CHAPTER 25

Later that week, Leo left his apartment to go for a drink at a local bar close to his apartment. He saw Ivan going into one of the buildings with someone. He did a double take. "Oh my God." It looked like the doctor's ex-wife, Donna. He stayed out of sight until they came out. Sure enough, it was her. "The Bitch!!" Who in the hell had fallen off that cliff? He went to the library close by before he went to the bar. He knew they kept newspapers a few days old. He started looking at newspapers from a couple of days ago until he found what he was looking for. The woman who fell from the cliff was in the obituary section and it said her name was Sandy Grant. They had a picture of her and he couldn't believe it. She looked just like Donna. Shit, they looked exactly alike. He left the library for the bar by his apartment, very upset. He wondered if Bill knew this. If he did, he would be after him. He sat at the table by himself and ordered a double bourbon. He waved at the bartender for another drink. He took a big swig of that and saw Jeff Ellis, one of his neighbors from his building come in.

Jeff came over, "mind if I join you Leo?"

"Sure, sit down, Jeff"

They both started talking and drinking. Leo was well on his way after his double bourbons. He started bad-mouthing Donna as usual.

> "You know, Jeff, someone actually offered me money to take our manager, Donna out, permanently."

> "Really," Jeff said. "But I didn't think it was worth it so I didn't bother. I sure could have used the money though."

Jeff thought that was information that might come in handy to know whenever he got in trouble again with the law. They continued talking and eventually staggered back to their apartment building.

> "Keep what I told you under your hat, Jeff."

> "Of course."

CHAPTER 26

A week later Ramon called the lieutenant from the interrogation room.

> "Lieutenant, I think we have a break in the Sandy Grant case. Can you come into the interrogation room now?"

> "I'll be right in Ramon."

Ramon met him outside the door to fill him in.

> "One of the tenants in Donna's apartments, Jeff Ellis, attempted to rob a liquor store this morning. He was caught and brought in for questioning. He tells the arresting officer he has useful information regarding the woman who fell in the ravine. He's willing to tell us if he can get a break in sentencing for robbing the liquor store."

> "Ramon, we need to record this. Make sure the audio visual is on. I'll go in there now and see him. Give me a high sign when everything is turned on. Has he been Mirandized?"

> "Yes lieutenant."

The lieutenant went in an introduced himself.

"Would you like anything to drink before we get started Mr. Ellis?"

"Maybe later."

The lieutenant saw Ramon give him the high sign and also saw the recording light come on in the room. He motioned for Ramon to come in.

"Mr. Ellis, please tell us what you know."

"Can you reduce my sentence if I tell you what I know, lieutenant?"

"There is a very good possibility, but it must be the absolute truth. If it's not the truth, then we cannot help you. Do you understand?"

"Yes, I do."

"Very well, go ahead."

"A tenant in my apartment building, a Leo Garcia, told me someone offered to pay him a significant amount of money to kill our apartment owner and manager, Donna Collins."

"Mr. Ellis, did he say who offered to pay him?"

"No, he didn't say." "Did Mr. Garcia say he took the money?"

"He said he did not, it wasn't worth the trouble. He just forgot about the whole thing, he didn't want to get involved."

"Thank you for your help, Mr. Ellis we will get back to you as soon as we can regarding your sentencing."

The lieutenant said to Ramon and Ted, "Pick up Leo and let's question him again."

CHAPTER 27

The detectives went to Leo's apartment. Ramon knocked on the door and Leo opened it.

"What is it this time?"

"We have further questions for you Leo, please come with us to the station." They Mirandized him and put him in their car and took him to the police station. Ramon called the lieutenant and told him they were bringing Leo in.

"Ramon when you come in make sure the audio visual is on. We want a recording on this."

The lieutenant walked into the interrogation room and sat across from Leo. Ramon and Ted remained in the room.

"Good afternoon Leo. We meet again. Leo, we have a statement from a reliable source that you told him someone offered to pay you to kill Donna Collins, but you declined. The source will testify to this. Who offered to pay you, Leo?"

Leo sat there silent.

"If you don't tell us Leo, I can assure you that you will spend the rest of your life in a maximum-security prison for murder or worse."

Leo sat there thinking, not saying a word. He thought, maybe it would be safer for him to tell the truth to the lieutenant. He could only hope that they would believe him. He'd rather have the police after Bill instead of Bill after him.

"Alright lieutenant. Dr. Bill Townsend paid me to kill Donna Collins."

"How much did he offer to pay you?"

"Two months back rent."

"How did he know that you were two months behind in your rent Leo?"

"I ran into Dr. Townsend at a local liquor store in San Pedro. I told him his wife was getting ready to evict me. I was two months behind in rent. He asked me what the total came to and I told him. He said that he could help me with that. We met at Charlie's Café on the corner down the street twenty minutes later. He showed me an envelope full of cash. He told me to count it. I did and it was the total amount I owed for rent. The doctor said it was mine but he wanted me to do something for it. I asked him what it was and he told me to take care of his wife, Donna, permanently. I told him that I would."

"Then what happened?" asked the lieutenant.

"I went to her house and parked my car on the street. Bill told me if she was home, she usually parked her car on the driveway by the house. I didn't see a car so I assumed she wasn't home. I walked up the steep slope to the top. Bill had told me the thick vegetation on the slope would

125

provide excellent cover for me. When I reached the top, I caught a glimpse of Donna, but I guess it was that other woman. She was standing right on the edge of the cliff, her blonde hair blowing in the wind. I was surprised to see her since I hadn't seen her car, but maybe she had put it in the garage. It looked like she was in some kind of a trance. But, I swear lieutenant, I didn't push that woman over the cliff. Someone else did. Suddenly I saw someone's hand shoot out and push her. But I couldn't see who it was through all that vegetation."

"Then what did you do Leo?"

"I waited a few minutes hoping whoever was there was gone and then went slowly down the steep grade to the street, got in my car as quickly as I could and drove away. Whoever else was up there had to have come from the opposite direction, more from the house, not from the street."

"Are you willing to take a lie detector test for us Leo?"

"Yes, lieutenant if it will help me."

"Good. Ramon, let's get it set up right now for Leo."

"Leo, one question, has Dr. Townsend tried to contact you at all after this happened?"

"No, sir."

"Do you know where he is, Leo?"

"No I don't."

While Leo was waiting for his test results he was thinking.

> "I wonder who actually pushed that woman off the cliff? Did they think it was Donna or that other woman?"

It was so hard to tell the difference, they looked so much alike. Leo's test results came back in a couple of hours.

> "Leo, you passed with flying colors. You can leave now, but please do not leave the area in case we have more questions. Thank you again for your cooperation. The lieutenant decided not to press charges against Leo for attempted murder. He knew an attorney would find the case weak and it would be a waste of time. Leo could always say he had a change of heart and changed his mind. "However, I am going to put a restraining order against you, Leo, regarding Donna. Believe me, if I hear you have come within 100 feet of her or have caused any trouble, we will lock you up so fast it will make your head spin. Is that clear Leo?"

> "Yes sir."

> "If you have any concerns, you are to contact the new property manager, Ivan. Is that clear?"

> "Yes lieutenant."

> "Let this be a lesson to you. This could have gone the other way for you. You could be serving many years in a maximum-security cell or worse. Please stay out of trouble! This could have gone the other way and have been very bad for you. Also Leo, what size shoe do you wear?"

"A size 11."

"Leo, please let us know immediately if you hear from Dr. Townsend again. Your life may be in danger. Thank you for your cooperation. You may go now."

The lieutenant asked Ramon to check Dr. Townsend's bank records, especially around the date the doctor had met with Leo.

"See if he withdrew an amount equal to what he gave Leo or higher."

Ramon got back to the lieutenant regarding Bill's bank account right away.

"Lieutenant he had a substantial amount withdrawn. It was enough to cover the two months back rent for Leo and also some extra probably to cover his trip back to Portland. The date of the withdrawal was the same as the date he met with Leo at Charlie's Café."

"Good work Ramon."

"Yes sir."

CHAPTER 28

"Mrs. Collins, this is lieutenant McClary. I would like to stop by again and update you on the development of the Sandy Grant case. Do you have time today?"

"Yes, I do. I will be home all morning."

"I'll be there shortly."

She greeted him at the door. "Coffee lieutenant, or anything to drink?"

"Coffee sounds fine. Mrs. Collins, Leo Garcia, a tenant at one of your apartment buildings has confessed to the following. Your ex-husband, Dr. Townsend, gave Leo the two months back rent as an incentive to kill you. Leo intended to do so, but someone was ahead of him and pushed Sandy Grant off the cliff into the ravine, probably thinking it was you. We have a warrant out for Dr. Townsend for attempted murder, murder, and conspiracy to commit murder. We were unable to locate him in California and believe he may have returned to Portland, which he did. My detectives went to look for him there, but we just missed him and now believe that he may be heading back to California. We found someone booked on a plane, from Portland to California a few days ago by the name of Peter Townsend. We are checking this out to see if there is any significance to the name. Does that name sound familiar to you at all?"

"No, lieutenant."

"I will keep you updated on where Bill is and when we arrest him. I wanted you to be aware of the situation and if you have any information, or should hear from him please call me immediately. If we find out that he did return to California I will assign you 24/7 police protection to you immediately. We feel you may be at risk and in danger Mrs. Collins. If you are afraid or sense anything abnormal, I want you to call me any time, right away. I strongly suggest you stay with your father until we arrest him. Does Bill know where your father lives?"

"No lieutenant, they avoided each other like the plague.

CHAPTER 29

Before Bill flew to California he went to see his brother, Paul Townsend in a rehab facility in Portland for drug addiction. He had never told anyone about Paul because he felt it would reflect badly on him. His father had a trust fund set up for him that would take care of Paul's expenses for life at the facility. When

When Bill entered his room he said, "Hi Paul."

They talked briefly and had been close growing up.

> "I brought you a few rolls of coins for the vending machine, Paul. I know you like those goodies."

> "Thanks Bill."

> "I'll put them in your nightstand."

Bill opened the drawer of his nightstand and placed the coins there. He saw Paul's driver's license in the drawer and when Paul wasn't looking he put Paul's driver's license in his pocket. Bill thought he would borrow it to use for his California trip. Just to be on the safe side in case anyone was looking for him. There wasn't much difference between them in the picture and the ages were not that far off. He didn't think he would have a problem.

Bill called a cab early the next morning for the airport. He used Paul's driver's license for identification at the airport and there was no problem at all. He was on his way back to California to keep his promise he made to himself to take care of Donna, permanently, once and for all.

Bill arrived at the Los Angeles Airport (LAX) around 11:00a.m. The flight had been short and bumpy. He took his carry-on bag into the restaurant at the airport. He was hungry and wanted something to eat and, definitely, something to drink. A hamburger and a couple of stiff drinks were just what he needed. After he left the restaurant, Bill went to the motel and picked up his FedEx package from the front desk registration which they were holding for him until he arrived. He turned on the television. Nothing exciting was on the news. He would rest a bit and wait until dark before taking off to Donna's place. He laid out his gun, checked the magazine and the action and put the gun in his coat pocket.

Bill had carefully replayed his plan over and over again in his mind. Leo had apparently pushed the wrong woman off the steep cliff thinking it was Donna. She and Donna looked exactly alike. When Bill was with Donna for a short time he knew Leo had a very bad reputation at the apartment buildings. All of the tenants knew Leo disliked Donna intensely. He was always causing her trouble and making her life miserable. Bill knew the police were aware of this. There was no doubt in his mind that Leo would become a person of interest in the fatal fall of the wrong woman. Bill didn't think anyone could prove he had paid Leo two months back rent to get rid of Donna.

To avoid suspicion when he withdrew the money from the bank, he withdrew more than enough money to not only pay Leo, but also to pay for his trip back to Portland. Now if something bad were to happen to Donna, Leo could very well be charged with a double homicide. Bill glanced out the window in his room. It was getting very dark. He smiled. It was time to go.

When Ramon and Ted returned to California they called several cheap motels in San Pedro they didn't have any luck, until the fifth try. A Paul Townsend registered there yesterday. Ramon and Ted sped off with an adrenaline high to the motel. It was dark when Ramon and Ted pulled up to the registration desk and parked. Ramon showed the clerk his badge and then a picture of Bill.

"Do you recognize this man?"

"Sure do. That's Paul Townsend."

"Bull's-eye!!"

Ramon asked that the desk clerk to please take them his room number. Ramon and Ted pulled out their guns, checked the magazines and the action. Ramon told the desk clerk to knock on the door. They told the clerk to stand off to the side. No answer. They knocked again. Same thing.

Ramon said loudly, "We have an electrical problem in your room and have to come in. Please open the door!"

Ramon then took the master key from the clerk and told him to stand back and he opened the door. Empty. Bill was not there. Ramon called the lieutenant. "Lieutenant, we found Bill's motel but must have just missed him. He had gone out."

"I will warn Donna right away, Ramon."

With Bill in the area she was in grave danger. Ramon asked the clerk not to mention to Bill that they had been there asking about him. Ramon also wanted to see if a car license plate was registered in his name so they could put out an APB. There was no registered license plate number on the rental car at the motel.

The lieutenant called Mrs. Collins at her home. He just got her voicemail and left a message.

"Mrs. Collins, this is Lieutenant McClary, please call me as soon as you can. It's extremely urgent."

He then called her father.

"Mr. Taylor, this is Lieutenant McClary. I'm trying to reach your daughter, Mrs. Collins. Do you know where she is?"

"Yes lieutenant, she has been in Catalina for a couple of days and is probably on the boat right now coming home."

"If you hear from her Mr. Taylor, please have her call me right away. I've tried her cell phone, but she probably has it turned off. Thank you, Mr. Taylor."

He knew that Donna was at risk. Her safety was a major concern. He hoped they weren't too late.

Donna took the last boat leaving from Catalina to come home in the evening. It was getting darker earlier now and she was anxious to get home. Ever since the annulment with Bill she was still afraid and apprehensive about coming home alone, especially in the dark, to an empty house. Bill was so unpredictable. He had threatened her several times and could be violent. She knew he had a gun and that worried her. He was mentally and physically abusive and was worse after he had been drinking. She was glad she had a restraining order out on him due to her attorney's insistence, but doubted in his case it would do much good.

As she drove up the long winding driveway she noticed the pool lights were on. This only happened if there was a security breach. Apprehensive, she left the car running as she reached the top of the driveway. Her eyes suddenly caught something large by the pool. She knew the workmen had left some debris there as they were doing some work on the deck but this was bigger. Oh my God, it looked like a body. She grabbed her cell phone and turned it on. She saw that she had missed a call from Lieutenant McClary on his cell phone. She called him back and he answered right away when he saw who was calling. She sounded frantic.

> "Lieutenant, I just pulled up to my home and I think something bad has happened by my pool. I'm afraid to get out of the car. Please come right away!"

He could hear the panic in her voice.

> "I'm on my way, Donna. Lock your car doors and do not get out of the car until I get there."

She knew it would take him at least twenty minutes.

While she waited for the Lieutenant it occurred to her that it could be someone she knew by the pool that might need help and not an intruder. Just in case, she took the concealed gun which David had kept in the car for her. She removed the safety and walked cautiously towards the pool with the gun held unsteadily in front of her.

"Oh no!" She gasped when she saw it was Bill by the pool.

"Don't move! I have a gun on you Bill and I won't hesitate to shoot you!"

Dead silence. She noticed a gun handle protruding from his coat pocket. He must have fallen over the debris and knocked himself out. He lay right at the edge of the pool. She thought, why couldn't he have just fallen in the pool and drown?

Donna was shaking so badly she could barely hold her gun. She knew Bill had come to kill her. Would this ever end?

She stood there thinking "Oh, what the hell," she said under her breath.

Donna put her gun in her coat pocket and grabbed the skimmer net by the pool. She didn't want to get too close to Bill. He scared the hell out of her. Trembling, she placed the pole part of the skimmer net on his back and gave a little push. Bill slid gracefully into the pool without even a splash. She put the skimmer net down where she found it and walked quickly back to her car. She got in and locked the doors her eyes never left the pool while she waited for the lieutenant. Finally, she could hear the sound of distant sirens coming.

Suddenly flashing lights came up the driveway. Thank goodness he was here. She saw the lieutenant draw his gun when he got out of his car. He motioned to her to stay in her car.

When he returned she said, "What happened, Lieutenant?"

> "It's Bill. He was apparently snooping around and tripped on the debris by the pool. He knocked himself out and fell into the pool and drowned. It was an accidental drowning plain and simple."

Donna was visibly shaken. She looked so vulnerable. He just wanted to hold her.

> "Donna, please go into the house, try to relax and fix yourself a good, strong drink. It will take us a couple of hours to finish everything we have to do out here plus the paperwork. I'll come and let you know when we are done."

> "Thank you, Lieutenant."

When Donna went into her house a giant wave of relief swept over her. She sat her drink down and said a prayer that she would be forgiven for what she had done. She didn't know if that was possible but she could only hope. She felt she had no choice. Panicked, she felt she took the best defense available to her.

The lieutenant knocked on Donna's door when they were finished.

> "Everything is taken care of Donna. The body has been removed. You know, Donna, it was a good thing that you were not at home earlier. Bill was obviously up to no good. He must have left his car in the street and walked up so you wouldn't see a car at the house. He was obviously planning on surprising you Donna. It's a good thing you didn't come home any earlier. He definitely was up to no good." Donna sat there in silence, still very traumatized. "What are your plans now, donna?"

> "Well, the workmen will have the deck completed by the end of the week since the weather has improved and they will start building the retaining wall right away. I don't want this to be an issue when I sell the place. I'm meeting with a realtor this week to list it. I want out of here as soon as possible. There are too many bad memories. I'll stay at my Dad's until I find something permanent. I'm hoping to get lucky and find a townhouse in the area as nice as the one I had before all this mess happened in my life. I loved my other one."

The lieutenant said, "Donna, you are in no condition to stay here by yourself tonight. I'm going to drive you to your father's house. But first call him and let him know we are coming."

> "Thank you so much lieutenant."

Before they left, they sat in the study and had a drink to calm their nerves.

When they were driving to her father's house, the lieutenant said,

> "I'm so glad you're okay Donna. Please let me know if you need anything?"

> "I will lieutenant."

He walked Donna to her father's door and said goodnight to both of them. He thought they needed some time to relax together. He couldn't stop thinking about Donna. She had been through too much. Things might have turned out a lot differently if she had arrived home any earlier from Catalina.

The police found a loaded gun in Bill's coat pocket when he was taken from the pool. Thank god everything worked out for the best and she was finally safe. The lieutenant was hoping Donna might be at the same fundraiser he was going to in a few weeks. He knew she went to these things all the time. There was something about her beautiful blue eyes that fascinated him.

CHAPTER 30

At the detectives weekly meeting the lieutenant brought everyone up to date on all the outstanding cases. It was a relief for the lieutenant to tell everyone that the Sandy Grant case was solved and closed. When the meeting was over he called Ramon and Ted in to thank them again for their outstanding work.

"There is one other thing we need to clear up."

"What is that, lieutenant?" Ramon said.

"We need to find out who Paul Townsend is. I have a feeling that he may be a relative of Bill's that we were not aware of. Could you please call the telephone number that was on Paul's driver's license that Bill was using, first, and then check out the address? Let me know what you find."

Ramon spoke to the lieutenant the next day.

"The telephone number is a rehab facility for drug users and also has permanent housing for patients there. I spoke with their director and he told me that Paul was Bill's brother and lived there permanently."

"I told him about Bill's drowning and said it was a pool accident. The director said he would prefer to

140

talk to Paul about it first as Bill and Paul were close as brothers. He also said the father had a trust fund set up for Paul for his lifetime because he felt he was unable to take care of himself for any length of time because of his addictions. So money is not a problem for Paul."

"Thank you, Ramon that is a relief. We will send Paul our condolences, and again, you and Ted did an outstanding job."

"Thank you, lieutenant. Please return Paul's driver's license also."

CHAPTER 31

A month later, Donna's house on the hill closed escrow. Donna had put everything she cared about in temporary storage until she and her Dad found a new place for her. She drove up the driveway to her father's house and opened the door a little.

"Woof woof."

"Where is that big guard dog?"

Murphy, his boxer came flying down the stairs overjoyed to see her. He went into his rumba dance and his stubby tail was going a hundred miles a minute.

Don came down the stairs. "What is all the commotion?"

"You know Dad you really should lock your front door."

"Hah! Murphy would kill them."

"You mean he would kiss them to death, don't you?"

Don was thrilled about the big house closing. Donna was going to be with him and Murphy for a while until the final inspection was completed on her beautiful new townhouse. He could hardly wait to surprise her. She had no idea he had already found her a beautiful new

townhouse. He and Murphy would cheer her up.
Murphy loved it when Donna was there and always went
to find his tennis ball or a squeaky toy. He liked to look at
himself in the downstairs mirror when he had a ball or
toy in his mouth.

Don still missed David. That whole thing was unfortunate
but then this Bill, what a mess he was. Don never did like
him and didn't trust him. Don always said that Bill had
shifty eyes and would never look directly at you. He was
glad to see him permanently out of his daughter's life in
more ways than one.

The next week when Donna came down for breakfast she
could sense her Dad was excited by something.

> "Honey, I have a little surprise for you this
> morning. Don't plan anything and I'll show you
> after you're dressed."

> "I'll hurry Dad, I'm dying to know what it is."

They left the house when she was ready.

> "Where are we going?"

> "You'll see."

They got in the car and drove a short distance from her
Dad's place and parked.

> "Here we are, sweetie."

She saw the most beautiful new townhome complex in a
gated community and she could see the ocean.

"Welcome home, it's all yours!"

"I can't believe it! Can we go inside now?"

She gave him a big hug and kiss.

"Of course, we can."

He gave her the key and she opened the door.

She heard "Come in, come in."

"Who is that Dad?"

"That's Henry. I thought you needed some new company and he certainly is an improvement over your last."

Henry was a handsome large green parrot with yellow trim. Henry started laughing when he heard Donna laugh.

"Parrots are so much company, Donna. Henry stayed with Murphy and me for a couple of days before I brought him here yesterday. He and Murphy really get along. One day when Murphy got carried away squeaking his favorite toy, Henry went into hysterics. He was laughing so hard he fell off his perch."

Donna asked "Was he okay?"

"Oh sure. He's a real character. He even thought it was funny."

CHAPTER 32

A few weeks later the lieutenant was at the fund raiser that he thought Donna might be attending also.

He spotted her right away and said, "Donna, small world isn't it?"

"It certainly is nice to see you again Lieutenant, especially under much better circumstances."

"Donna, please call me Stephen. I hope that's okay. I feel like we know each other by now."

"Of course, Stephen."

"Can I get you a drink, Donna?"

"Yes, that sounds good."

"I think the beverage of choice is champagne. Is that okay?"

"That is fine."

"I'll bring us a few appetizers, too. How is everything going Donna?"

"A lot better, thank you."

"Have you found a new townhouse yet?"

"Yes, and it is beautiful."

They chatted easily for a couple of hours discovering they had a lot in common. She could feel the attraction between them. She had heard he was a widower with no children. After they had talked for a while. He said, "Donna, I don't mean to be too forward but would you consider having dinner with me one night?"

Donna thought to herself. Okay girl, you've been through the ringer twice now, let's don't get carried away. Do you really want to go there? Then she looked up at his rugged good looks and smiled. "I would love to have dinner with you Stephen."

"How about this Saturday night?"

"That sounds good"

"I'll pick you up about 7:00 and I promise no flashing lights or sirens."

Donna laughed.

"I'm glad you accepted my invitation Donna. I wasn't sure. You've been through so much."

"I'm looking forward to it Stephen."

She kept reminding herself to just take it nice and slow.

Stephen said, "I'm really anxious to see your new place. He could hardly wait for next Saturday. Donna gave him her new address.

He chose a nice surf-n-turf restaurant that specialized in seafood and steaks. Their dinner was excellent and they accompanied it with a fine bottle of wine. They liked the atmosphere which was dark and romantic. They were in no hurry to eat and were enjoying each other over their drinks. Stephen was good company. They talked about everything and seemed to like the same things. When he took her home, she asked him to come in.

The minute she opened the door, Henry yelled, "Come in, Come in!!"

> "Stephen, I want you to come and meet my parrot Henry. He was a housewarming gift from my father, Don."

Stephen liked Henry right away and started paying a lot of attention to him.

> "Stephen, what would you like to drink? I have a very good after dinner liqueur if that sounds good?"

> "That sounds great. Donna, I love your place. You have so many beautiful things. Everything is so exotic. Are they all from your travels?"

She smiled.

> "Oh, a little here and there but mostly local."

They sat on the couch talking and sipping their drinks. He loved looking at her with those deep blue eyes.

> "Donna, tell me more about Catalina."

> "Well Stephen, Catalina provides a great release for me from my hectic schedule here at home. I turn off my cell phone the minute I leave and don't turn it back on until I return home. In case of an emergency the hotel can always reach me in Catalina."

"Where do you stay?"

"I think it is the best hotel there and it's right on the main street, steps from water. The staff is wonderful. They always try to give me my favorite room. And when I arrive they have a big basket full of cheese, crackers, and all sorts of other goodies, as well as a bottle of fine wine waiting for me. They have a complimentary breakfast consisting of freshly baked scones and muffins and all kinds of fresh fruit, orange juice and fresh coffee. They also have a beautiful sun deck at the top of the hotel overlooking the water. And in the winter, they even have suites with a fireplace available, but most of all I love the shopping there. Almost all of the things you like in my townhouse are from the local artisans and craftsmen from the exquisite shops there. There are a few restaurants I go to that are my favorites that specialize in superb seafood and steaks, and the drinks aren't bad either. There is actually something for everyone there but I like the shopping and fine dining the best."

"It sounds wonderful Donna. I can see why you enjoy it so much."

Stephen said, "I had a great time with you tonight Donna."

"I like being with you too Stephen."

He was thinking of all the things he wanted to do to her but didn't want to press his luck. "Well," he said, "I had better go."

He was feeling a little more confident and said, "Would you like to do this again?"

"Yes, I would."

"Could I call you next week?"

"Of course," she said.

He gave her a light kiss on her mouth.

"Goodnight Donna."

"Goodnight Stephen."

Stephen called her the next week. He was hoping she wouldn't think he appeared too anxious.

"Hi Donna, it's Stephen."

"Oh, I'm glad you called Stephen."

His heart jumped.

"Would you like to go out this Saturday again?"

"Yes, that sounds lovely."

"Same time."

"Okay, bye."

"Bye."

Neither one of them were big phone talkers and she liked that.

Stephen picked her up on time Saturday. This time they went to a well-known little Italian restaurant not far from

149

her townhouse. It was quiet and intimate and perfect for their night out together. They touched glasses and enjoyed their drinks and the soft music. The restaurant was known for its Italian specialties and they enjoyed it immensely with a bottle of good red wine. When he took her home, they sat in his car for a while talking. She was thinking. Just remember to take it nice and slow. Then he leaned in and the proper kiss from the last time went to a deeper one with a lot of tongue action. He was so attractive and was beginning to turn her on. When he moved his hand down to her breasts she asked, "Stephen, would you like to come in for an after-dinner drink?"

Stephen gulped. "Yes, I would."

Donna had a special liqueur she had just bought and she thought he might like it. He sat on her couch while she fixed their drinks.

"I think you'll like this Stephen."

She sat down next to him, they touched glasses and they sat close together.

"What do you think?"

"I like it."

She could feel the desire building between them. Stephen set down his drink and reached for her, holding her tight against his body. He ached for her. She could feel him becoming aroused. She knew he wanted her and could feel his hardness starting to press against her body.

"I want you so much Donna."

She touched his cheek and whispered in his ear.

"I want you too, Stephen."

150

Stephen asked, "Shall we go into your bedroom?"

Donna said, "I think we'd better."

She stood up and took him by his hand into her bedroom. They quickly started removing each other's clothing until they were naked and fell on the bed. Donna lay on her back thinking. Well so much for taking things nice and slow.

Stephen kissed her intimately then moved his hand down between her legs. She spread them wider and he started penetrating her with one and then two fingers. Donna wanted him badly and didn't need any more foreplay now. She hadn't had any sex for several months. She wanted to feel him inside her. She began moving her hips against him moaning softly. She could feel him becoming harder and harder. She wrapped her fingers around his erection and she could feel him starting to penetrate her.

She cried out, "Now Stephen, NOW!"

He thrust into her groaning as he moved in and out, slowly, then deeper and deeper. Donna began writhing with desire. She wanted him so badly. Then he began to move faster and faster. He kept thrusting in and out, over and over again, faster and faster, until she cried out. "Oh my god Stephen. Don't stop. Don't stop!"

They were both panting hard with desire and came to a climax simultaneously.

They lay back close together catching their second wind.

Stephen said, "I hope I didn't take advantage of you Donna?"

She touched his arm.

> "Are you kidding Stephen? It may have been the other way around. I've never been with a lieutenant before, and one in charge of homicide to boot!"

He gave a low chuckle and thought how lucky he was to have met this woman. He hadn't felt this way about anybody in a long, long time. He felt her fingers touch his neck affectionately.

> "You know Stephen, I can't seem to get enough of you."

She began moving her hand down his body until she reached what she was after. She began stroking him slowly. He moaned and said. "Donna you're killing me, but I love it. Your hand is so soft."

She quickened her pace until she felt him becoming hard again then she moved on top of him. He pushed her upward so he could enter his full erection into her. She cried out. "Oh yes Stephen. Yes."

When he began to penetrate her, she began moaning loudly and undulating with desire. She started riding him until she was out of control and kept coming over and over again. They both cried out and reached an explosive climax together.

They lay back exhausted together.

Stephen said, "I hope I'll be able to walk normally tomorrow."

Donna laughed, "I was just thinking the same thing."

"You know I love being with you Donna. I think we truly have something special. You know I think about you all the time."

"I feel that way too Stephen. By the way, I'm having my dad and close friends, Sheila and Bob over for dinner this coming Saturday. I'd love for you to come."

"I would like that Donna."

She smiled at him and said.

"You can stay over if you like."

Stephen thought he had just died and gone to heaven. Just the thought of spending a vigorous weekend in bed with her made him crazy.

Donna had been planning a dinner at her new place with her father, and Sheila and Bob. She was glad that Stephen could join them. She called her father after Stephen had left and told him Stephen would be joining everyone for dinner this coming Saturday. Don was delighted. She said, "Be sure and bring Murphy. He and Henry can entertain each other."

Donna thought about Stephen. She liked everything about him. Little did Stephen know he would have to overcome three major hurdles at dinner, her father, Murphy, and of course Henry.

When Donna was driving by her Dad's place the next day she noticed more cars than usual parked in front of his house. She was curious and parked her car in his driveway. She opened his door and went in.

"Yoo-hoo, anybody here?"

Murphy came flying out from the study to greet her.

"Hi big boy, I brought you a cookie."

"We are in the study, hon."

She thought who is we? Donna went into the study and she saw a couple and a very attractive lady playing cards with her Dad.

"We're playing bridge and just getting ready to take a break." Don introduced her to the other three. "Donna this is Connie and Jack and his wife June. This is my one and only beautiful daughter, Donna." It looked like they were having a good time. She saw another table set up in the study with drinks and all kinds of appetizers. She noticed how pretty Connie was and wondered if she and her Dad had anything going on. She never thought of him as having any kind of relationships, but why not? He was a very handsome and attractive man.

Don said, "Lets' all have something to drink, everybody help yourselves."

Murphy ran to get a squeaky toy and show off.

"Everybody lives close by in the neighborhood, hon, and we all love to play bridge. We have been alternating at each other's houses playing once a month. I think bridge is the best card game there is, and who do you think came up with it? I think the Chinese, who else?"

Donna thought as she was driving home she would have to question her Dad a little more about this Connie. They seemed to really like each other. It looked like they were having a lot of fun. She wondered if they went out to dinner and enjoyed other activities as well. Well, why not? It was good for him.

Donna called her Dad the next morning. "Okay Dad, why haven't you mentioned Connie to me before? She is very attractive and seems very nice. Anything going on I need to know about?"

"Not a thing sweetheart, I haven't known her very long and we are just good friends."

"How did you meet her?"

"Jack and June introduced me to her at one of their dinner parties. We all seem to have a great time together."

"I'm just snoopy Dad. I just like to take care of you like you like to take care of me. I wish I set a better example with my love life but, unfortunately, it didn't work out that way."

"It wasn't your fault sweetheart, and from what you told me I think Stephen may be the right one. I don't think they make them any better than Stephen."

"You know you're right Dad. Sometimes I can be such a slow learner. I'm so glad you're my Dad. You always pick me up and put me on the straight and narrow."

"That's what Dad's are for honey."

"Dad, you know if you would like to bring someone to dinner this Saturday, please do. Maybe bring your friend Connie?"

"No, I'm okay sweetie, but perhaps another time."

Donna was not a cook by any means and she knew it but she loved to entertain. She used a little trick of hers that was a little bit sneaky about the cooking part, but it seemed to work. She had a comfortable arrangement with the owner of one of her favorite restaurants close by. They made all her favorite dishes and appetizers and put them in some of Donna's serving dishes, which she left there on a permanent basis. She had several sets of the dishes there so they were always on hand when she ordered something special for company. They would use her serving dishes and deliver them early to her house before it was time for guests to arrive. That way all she had to do was heat everything up before serving time. Voila! Everyone always raved about her dinners. Donna always pretended to be a little shy about the compliments and said, "Thank you, I'm glad you enjoyed it." God forbid if someone asked her for a recipe, but if they did, she conveniently got busy and forgot about the question.

Donna called her favorite restaurant owner, Andre, to give him her dinner selection for Saturday.

"Hi Donna, what can I make for you and your guests?"

156

"Let's see, Andre, there will be five of us. Better make enough for eight in case they want seconds. How about your wonderful shrimp risotto with the homemade bread, a salad with more of the good things in it and not so much lettuce, and creamed spinach? I'll do dessert if they want it."

"You got it. What time do you want it delivered?"

She told him.

When Saturday night arrived, Stephen arrived first, then Sheila and Bob. Introductions were made. Donna took everyone's drink orders. Stephen helped her make them at the bar and they served them. Donna's father and Murphy arrived fifteen minutes later. When Murphy heard Henry yell. "Come in. Come in," he made a beeline to see Henry immediately. Murphy had his favorite squeaky toy in his mouth and started going through all his antics, squeaking his toy like crazy, and throwing it in the air and catching it. Henry went nuts and started laughing hysterically. When Murphy and Henry saw they had a captured audience they carried on even more.

Donna said to Stephen, "You didn't expect entertainment, tonight did you?"

Stephen started laughing and said.

"I love it."

Then they all started laughing. After a while Don said,

"Okay guys, time out. Murphy and Henry, you each get a treat. They would go on for hours like this if I let them."

157

Don said, "Sometimes Henry will get so carried away laughing and he will fall off his perch. He even thinks that's funny."

Everyone loved their dinner and ate everything, even seconds and were too full for dessert.

"Thank goodness." Donna thought.

She needed a time out. They all adjourned to the living room and had an after dinner drink and continued enjoying each other's company. Murphy was sticking close to Stephen. Stephen kept rubbing his ears and talking to him. Donna had a spare toy box for Murphy downstairs and Murphy suddenly ran to it looking for something. He came back to Stephen with one of his tennis balls in his mouth and dropped it on Stephen's lap. Don started laughing.

"Stephen that's quite a compliment. He doesn't do that unless he thinks you're pretty special."

Stephen said, "I love dogs. I think they sense when you really like them."

Don looked at his daughter. She looked radiant beaming at Stephen and Murphy. Mission accomplished. He thought, thank goodness she is back to being herself again. He hadn't seen her this happy in a long, long time.

Before Sheila and Bob left, Sheila caught Donna in the kitchen and told her how much they liked Stephen. Sheila said, "We will have the two of you over to our house for dinner soon."

"That would be great, Sheila." Donna said.

"I really like Stephen, too. I think he's very special.

Everyone had a great evening and it was late when they left. Donna covered Henry's cage so he could get a good night's sleep after Murphy and Don went home. They were the last to leave. Stephen helped Donna clean up and put things away.

Donna said, "Stephen would you like to go to bed now?"

He looked at her with a devilish smile and said,

"I'll race you up the stairs."

Donna smiled and thought to herself that things were definitely looking up. You never know she thought, but this time she knew she did. After they made love again, they were just relaxing and enjoying the closeness of being together.

Donna was lying on her back staring at the ceiling.

Stephen said, "What are you thinking about now, Donna?"

"I was just wondering what color to paint this ceiling."

Stephen started laughing.

"Is that because when we are together you spend a lot of time on your back?"

"That will do it, Stephen."

CHAPTER 33

It was a typical sunny California day and the beautiful blonde-haired woman had had a good but tiring day shopping in San Pedro. She walked down by the waterfront. She went by the Breaker's 9 restaurant and decided she was hungry for some seafood and maybe a cocktail. She sat in the booth and ordered lunch. It felt good to just relax and look at the ocean view. A voice came from behind that sounded familiar and asked

"Can I buy you a drink?" She turned around and saw a face she immediately recognized. She put on a pleasant face and smiled.

"Hello. My name is David Collins."

She replied, "and I am Barbara Richards."

He asked, "Do you mind if I join you?"

"No, not at all." Thank goodness she did not see any sign of recognition in his eyes.

He couldn't stop staring at her blue eyes. They were the brightest blue. She was absolutely beautiful. The waiter came by and asked if she was finished with her lunch. She said yes and he removed the dishes.

"Would you like anything else?" the waiter asked.

David said "We'll have a couple of cocktails. What would you like Barbara?"

"A scotch and water sounds good."

"Make that two." David said.

They spent the next hour talking about things in general.

"Barbara, would you like to stop by my place for another drink?"

"Yes, I would."

"You can follow me in your car if you like. My apartment is close by."

"Sure."

Sandy felt odd, like she was in a fog like state. She didn't know why but she noticed he was no longer wearing a ring.

She followed him in his car to his place in San Pedro. His apartment was small, very cold and stark looking. There were no pictures at all.

David told her, "Make yourself comfortable."

Barbara sat on the couch and he joined her with the drinks. He was thinking,

"How lucky can one guy get?"

She was drop-dead gorgeous. David didn't realize how true the meaning of his words were.

He stood up and said, "Nature calls, I'll be right back."

He went into the bathroom. Barbara opened up her purse, took out a large capsule and broke it in half. She dropped the entire contents into David's drink gently swishing it around his glass. She quickly wiped the glass with a Kleenex from her pocket and stuck the tissue back into her purse. David returned to the sofa and sat close to her. She picked up her drink and raised her glass in a toast gesture. He did the same and they toasted each other. David gulped all of his drink down quickly then reached for Barbara, his hand moving towards her breast. All of a sudden, he was getting a little dizzy and started to feel light headed. He laid his head back on the back of the couch and started to say something but the words came out slurry. David started to get drowsy and was having a hard time keeping his eyes open. Barbara stood up and grabbed her purse.

"I guess you don't remember me David."

He looked at her in a daze.

"THE NAME IS SANDY GRANT!! Sweet dreams, David."

She saw a faint glimmer of recognition and then she saw his eyes turn to panic. He struggled to move towards her but fell back against the couch and passed out. Sandy was very careful when she came into his apartment not to touch anything. She knew they would dust for prints later. She drank the rest of her drink and tossed her empty glass into her purse. She would get rid of her glass later. Sandy covered the front door knob with a napkin from a nearby table and opened the door. She looked carefully outside and didn't see anyone. Sandy walked out into the bright sunshine and got into her little Toyota.

She drove to her new apartment the lieutenant had found for her in San Pedro, still in a daze.

The next day at the police station Lieutenant McClary motioned for Ramon and Ted to come into his office.

The lieutenant said, "We had a death in San Pedro yesterday and it's someone we know."

Ramon said, "Who was it, lieutenant?"

"David Collins."

"What happened lieutenant?"

"It appears he was by himself drinking a cocktail in his apartment. Forensics said there was a large quantity of a strong drug in his drink. The medical examiner said he never recovered. It wasn't the drug that killed him, but a massive heart attack. The crime scene team investigated but said that everything was as clean as a whistle. There was absolutely no sign of foul play. The case has been closed. I'll notify Donna and Sandy before they hear about it through the media or read about it in the newspapers."

CHAPTER 32

Stephen called Elliot Harper, the D.A.,

> "Elliott, I need to bring you up to date on a few items we discussed before. Shall we do an early dinner again?"

> "Sounds good to me Stephen."

> "How about Melvin's again? I love that place."

> "Sure, I'll make a reservation at my table. How about 6:00 o'clock again?"

> "See you there Elliott."

They met and ordered drinks first and then got down to business.

> "Elliott, first of all, Sandy Grant has been released from the hospital and is doing very well. Even the doctors are amazed. It's amazing how well she has recovered. She is truly a beautiful person inside as well as outside. I think my best detective, Ramon, has fallen head over heels for her. We had three suspects that looked good for pushing her over that cliff. David Collins, Dr. Bill Townsend, and Leo Garcia, a tenant in one of Donna Collins' apartment buildings. It turns out that Dr.

Townsend actually paid Leo Garcia to kill Donna Collins. However, when Leo went to push Donna over the cliff, someone was ahead of him and beat him to it. Leo didn't know who pushed her but took and passed a lie detector test with flying colors. Leo learned later from the newspapers that the woman was not Donna but a Sandy Grant, who was pushed. She looked enough like Donna to be her twin. We know it wasn't Dr. Townsend because he paid Leo to commit the crime for him. So that leaves David Collins. David had plenty of motive and opportunity. There was plenty of circumstantial evidence against David. David died recently from a heart attack. We have no evidence of foul play. So there you have it Elliott."

"What a story Stephen."

"Let's order, Elliott, I don't know about you, but I'm starving."

They both ordered the house specialty again, the dover sole with another martini. When Stephen returned to his office he called Josh Ryan, the medical examiner. He thanked Josh again for keeping everything under wraps until Sandy had been released from the hospital and they felt confident that it was David Collins that pushed her off the cliff.

Donna and Sheila met for lunch the next day.

Donna said, "Sheila, I have something to tell you."

"What is it?"

"I don't think it's been released yet but Stephen informed me that David was found dead in his apartment."

"What happened?"

Donna repeated the story that Stephen had told her.

"There was no indication of foul play."

"What do you think Donna?"

"I don't know. I didn't know he had a heart condition."

"Donna, Do you think that wandering eye might have finally caught up with him?"

"I think you could be right, Sheila. Please let Bob know. I know they were good friends."

"I will."

CHAPTER 33

Sandy felt so lucky just to be alive. She lost track of the many operations she went through, but they were finally over. She remembered the doctors and the plastic surgeon telling her she would still be as beautiful as she was before and feel like herself within six months. They put her together again from head to toe, piece by piece, which was no small feat. She felt whole again. The doctors had kept their word and she would never forget them. After she left David's apartment she could hardly wait to get home to her little apartment the lieutenant had found for her, in San Pedro. She felt like she was living a very bad dream and needed to lie down and rest.

When Stephen saw Sandy, he said, "I need to tell you something rather than have you read it in the newspapers."

"What is it Stephen?"

"David died recently from a heart attack."

"What happened?"

"He was alone having a cocktail in his apartment when it happened. The drink contained a strong drug, but it was actually the heart attack that killed

167

him. The case has been closed and there will be something in the paper about it soon. I just thought you should know."

"Thank you, for telling me, I appreciate it."

Sandy knew she would eventually sell her little boat. She did not want to go back to the marina again. She would feel uncomfortable and it just wouldn't be the same. She would keep her reliable little Toyota. She liked her little apartment and her neighbors were very friendly and nice to her. Sandy did some secretarial work on the side for the lieutenant's department and that helped her pay for her rent and expenses, temporarily. The doctors said that she could go back to work full-time, possibly by next month.

The lieutenant had not disclosed the information about Sandy's survival to anyone and that included his own department. Initially he felt it would be better for Sandy's recovery and safer for her if he kept it quiet. She agreed when he discussed it with her in the hospital. He didn't want to put her life in jeopardy again until they had the right suspect. He was glad he kept it quiet temporarily and let Sandy recover in peace. The lieutenant checked on her from time to time to see if she needed anything and she appreciated his concern.

After David's fatal heart attack, the lieutenant felt that Sandy was no longer in any danger. When she was released from the hospital he had taken her under his wing to help her adjust. He introduced her to Bob

Griffith, a good friend of his who had an apartment building in a safe and good area of San Pedro. A vacancy was available, which was unusual. The tenant had just been transferred to another state by his job so the timing worked out great. Bob liked having a full building with good tenants so he kept the rents stable. Everyone had been there for years. Sandy liked him immediately. He was in his sixties.

He said, "Sandy you will fit in perfectly here. We have a mixed age group and everybody gets along. It's one big happy family."

He showed her the available apartment which was downstairs. It was just perfect for her and she took it. Bob told her they were having a pot luck dinner on his patio Saturday night. All of the tenants would be there and were anxious to meet her. Apparently the "pot luck" was a monthly ritual. She could hardly wait. She was beginning to feel good again. Sandy felt she would be able to go back to work full-time in another month. In the meantime, the lieutenant had her doing some secretarial work for his department which helped pay the expenses. She would eventually sell her little boat. She didn't want to go back to the marina again or any other marina for that matter. Sandy liked being around more people now and was not so lonely. Sandy appreciated the lieutenant's concern. He was a good man and she felt safe knowing he was keeping an eye on her.

The lieutenant called Ramon into his office.

> "Ramon, I'm going to tell you something that has been kept quiet, purposely, after Sandy Grants' fall."

169

When he told Ramon she was alive, Ramon was speechless. He continued telling Ramon all of the details.

> "She has now been released from the hospital and I need your help. I check on Sandy from time to time just to be sure she is okay. But as you know, I am involved in meetings that take up too much of my time. I would like you to check on her if I am unavailable just for a few months. Would that be possible? What do you think Ramon?"

> "I'm more than happy to lieutenant."

> "Good, tomorrow I would like for you to meet her."

> "Yes sir, I would be happy to."

The lieutenant called Sandy and told her he would like to stop by for a few minutes late in the afternoon. He wanted her to meet someone.

She said, "Sure, lieutenant."

He and Ramon went to Sandy's apartment and the lieutenant introduced Ramon.

The lieutenant said, "Sandy, I would like Ramon to check on you from time to time, just until you feel like yourself again and are back on your feet." The lieutenant told her that Ramon was his very best detective. "When I'm tied up, I feel very comfortable with Ramon helping me."

> "I appreciate your concern lieutenant, but I will be fine."

The lieutenant wouldn't hear of it.

170

"Just for a little while Sandy."

When they left, Ramon said,

"I can't believe she survived that fall lieutenant! She is a beautiful woman."

> "I agree Ramon. She is doing remarkably well. She has therapy twice a week and also does special exercises a couple of days a week. She is getting there."

Sandy was thinking about how handsome Ramon was with his Latino good looks and was so nice. She noticed from habit that he didn't have a ring on his finger. The lieutenant had been unusually busy in his office, so he asked Ramon to fill in for him on Saturday and stop by and check on her. He did so. They were apparently having a pot-luck that night and Sandy invited him to stay.

When everyone was seated at the pot luck Bob stood up and said, "I'd like to make an announcement everyone and introduce our new tenant Sandy Grant. Sandy, stand up so everyone can see your pretty face."

> "Oh, Bob, I am so happy to be here with all of you and I would also like to introduce my special friend Ramon Ruiz."

Ramon stood and everyone clapped. The pot luck began.

Sandy felt just as comfortable and safe with Ramon as she did with the lieutenant. She wasn't looking for any kind of relationship now, maybe later when she was fully

171

recovered. But it was awfully nice to have a good friend like Ramon and he was so easy on the eyes. He thanked her for inviting him to the pot luck.

> "Ramon, if the lieutenant is going to be tied up for a while when you come by make sure it's our pot luck night and join us."

Ramon beamed. "I might take you up on that Sandy. I'm a single guy and not much of a cook. I would really enjoy that, thank you."

On the way back to his apartment, Ramon thought what a great evening that was. He liked all the tenants and the owner of the building too. They all seemed to enjoy his company also. He really liked Sandy and he felt good about seeing her. She was so nice. He couldn't believe all she had been through. He was glad the lieutenant asked him to help her.

At their next pot luck, Ramon stopped by his parent's Mexican restaurant, "La Puerta Abierta (The Open Door)," in San Pedro and picked up a large tray of enchiladas from his mother, Beatrice. His mother was very suspicious. Ramon had never done this before. She wanted to know exactly where he was taking her enchiladas, who would be there, etc, etc.

> "Mom you ask too many questions. I'm going to a pot luck dinner with friends and I want to impress everyone. You know nobody makes enchiladas as good as you do."

> "Oh Ramon."

His dad, Roberto, who handled the business part of the restaurant just smiled. He knew Ramon was up to something but knowing his wife, Beatrice, she would eventually find out. Ramon also stopped by a florist and picked out a small but colorful bouquet of flowers for Sandy. When he got to Sandy's, she heard him coming and opened the door.

"Oh Ramon, what did you bring?"

She was so excited and put the flowers in a vase with water right away.

"This is so nice of you! They are so beautiful."

He thought he saw a tear in her eye. She hugged him and gave him a little kiss on his cheek.

"And look at this tray of enchiladas. Everyone will go crazy over these."

Ramon just beamed.

"I'll heat these up now, Ramon, and then we can join everyone on the patio. When they went to the patio, everyone said, "Hi Ramon, we're so glad to see you again."

He felt like he had made so many new friends. The enchiladas went quickly and everyone loved them. Ramon and Sandy had a great time with everyone and spent a couple of hours talking and laughing about everything. Bob, the owner was so pleased and noticed Sandy was looking like she felt better and better each day. When they left, they said their goodbyes and everyone said, "See you soon Ramon. Remember, you can come over anytime, even before the next pot luck."

They all laughed. That made him feel so good. Ramon said goodnight to Sandy when they got back to her door. She gave him another hug and when he gave her a light kiss on the cheek, she thanked him again. She had never felt so happy.

The next day when Ramon was in the office, the lieutenant said to him,

> "I hear through the grapevine that you seem to be just what the doctor ordered for Sandy."

Ramon blushed.

> "I was thinking that she is looking stronger and stronger all the time lieutenant and her pain is a lot less too."

Ramon knew that the lieutenant had probably talked to Bob, the owner, since they were good friends.

> "Keep up the good work Ramon."

> "Yes sir."

> "Whatever you are doing, keep doing it! I think you have been helping Sandy's recovery immensely."

> "Thank you, lieutenant."

When Ramon saw Sandy again, he said, "Sandy, I know you liked the enchiladas so I am guessing that you are fond of Mexican food."

> "You're right Ramon. I love it."

"Well, when you are up to it I want to take you to my favorite Mexican restaurant."

"I am up for it now, Ramon, that is so nice of you. What is it called?"

"La Puerta Abierta in San Pedro. It's owned by my parents. It means The Open Door. That's where the enchiladas came from."

"I have heard many good things about this restaurant Ramon and I would love to go."

"Then we will. How about this Saturday night?"

"Sounds good, I can hardly wait and look forward to meeting your parents."

Ramon said goodnight. He too could hardly wait for Saturday.

When the lieutenant was in his office working he asked Ramon, again, how he was doing with Sandy.

Ramon smiled and said, "Couldn't be better Lieutenant."

"You look like you have put on a few extra pounds Ramon."

"I might have. I've been going to the apartment pot luck dinners."

The lieutenant smiled, "well, you look good and you could use a few pounds. Thank you for helping me out Ramon."

"You're welcome. If it's all right with you lieutenant I would like to keep doing it."

"That's fine, Ramon."

"Thank you, lieutenant."

"Let me know if it gets to be too much, Ramon."

"Yes sir. I can actually handle this in my spare time, so it's no problem at all lieutenant."

"Very well."

The lieutenant thought if he didn't know any better it looked like Ramon had a certain glow about him. The lieutenant smiled and said to no one in particular, "He seems to be acting differently, too, talking and smiling at everyone in the office and he has a little bounce in his step. Stephen thought I do believe Ramon is falling in love. He thought, I wonder if I have any quirky habits. I'll have to make sure I don't have any bounce in my step!

On Saturday night, Ramon took Sandy to "La Puerta Abierta," which was in a very nice neighborhood in San Pedro. It had been there for more than fifteen years with an established reputation as one of the best Mexican restaurants in town. When they walked in Sandy could hear the Mexican music playing softly in the background. The lighting was subdued and added to the romantic atmosphere. The floors were beautiful in a mosaic Mexican tile with colorful hand-painted Mexican furniture. The paintings that adorned the walls were all from famous Mexican artists. She felt like she had been transported south of the border.

"I think I recognize some of the paintings, Ramon."

"You probably do Sandy. They are very well known and do look authentic."

Beatrice and Roberto came to greet them immediately with open arms. Ramon had warned them ahead of time that Sandy was recovering from an accident so no bear hugs, etc. Sandy liked them immediately, they made her feel at home and very special.

Ramon pulled her chair out for her at their table which was set up especially for them. Roberto brought them his special margaritas for starters. Everything sounded good on the menu. She couldn't make up her mind. Sandy told Beatrice that all the people in her apartment were still raving about her enchiladas.

> "I'm happy to make you anything you like for your pot luck."

> "Thank you, Beatrice." Sandy said, "Ramon, will you surprise me and order for me?"

> "I can't make up my mind, it all sounds so delicious."

They had a superb dinner and drinks. Ramon kept an eye on Sandy and watched her like a hawk. Sandy hated to leave but Ramon noticed she was tiring quickly. They thanked Beatrice and Roberto, profusely, and said they could hardly wait to come back. Beatrice and Roberto remembered what Ramon had told them and gave Sandy a light hug and told her to hurry back. When Ramon took Sandy back to her apartment she could not stop telling him about what a wonderful evening she had and how much she liked his parents. He could tell she was exhausted, but happy, and that meant a lot to him. Ramon put his arms gently around her at the door and gave her a light kiss on her cheek. She was still so delicate and he didn't' want to hurt or scare her in any way.

"Thank you again Ramon for such a wonderful evening."

"You're welcome Sandy, I enjoyed it too. I'll call you in a few days."

Sandy went into her apartment and straight to her bedroom to lie down and relax. She thought about the evening and knew she had never been this happy. She felt like a new person. She knew it was because so many wonderful people really cared about her and she felt the same way about them. As she lay there, Sandy was thinking Ramon was such a gentleman and took such good care of her. What a difference from the men she met in bars. But then maybe the ones in bars were expecting to meet women like them. Who knows. She called the lieutenant and left him a message about how great Ramon was treating her.

Sandy had also read about David's death in the paper. Sandy still wasn't sure what happened to her in the restaurant that day, but the minute she heard David's voice behind her something snapped. Just like the mystery books she read, there was the opportunity and she took it. She had gotten rid of the evidence in her purse after she left. It had all seemed like a very bad dream that she didn't want to ever remember or relive again. She had put him out of her mind just like he had her, and that was the end of that.

Ramon was very close to his parents and he had a small but very nice house in a good part of San Pedro. It was very close to where his parents lived. He liked being close to them in case they needed him for anything. One night after he and Sandy had been to "La Puerta Abierta" again for dinner, he asked her if she would like to go for a little drive and see his house. She thought that would be great. When they drove up his driveway she noticed how beautiful the landscaping was. So many colorful flowers and trees.

"Ramon, this is beautiful. Do you do all the gardening yourself?"

"Usually Sandy, if I'm not on a really busy case. I enjoy it and find it relaxing. Let me show you the inside."

Sandy loved it. She couldn't believe how meticulous he was.

"My Mom helped me pick out some of the furnishings. That's not really my strong point."

"It's beautiful Ramon, and you even have a fireplace. I love that."

"Let me show you my patio in back."

The patio was lit with colorful lights and had comfortable patio furniture.

"Can I get you something to drink? How about a glass of wine?"

"Okay, but can we sit out here Ramon? It's such a clear night."

He brought them their wine and they talked about everything. Ramon thought maybe sometime soon she might want to stay over. He really didn't want her to go, but he didn't want to be too forward. He felt that they were heading in the right direction though. He would be patient and wait a little longer. Sandy was actually

179

thinking along the same lines but she wasn't sure if she was up to it yet. Ramon was terribly attractive and had probably been with many women. She didn't want to push it. Maybe she would mention it to her doctor next week when she had her physical. It sounded silly, but she was feeling so much better and she didn't want to slow down the healing process. Ramon was so sweet. She would play everything by ear for now, but she felt she could tell him anything and he would understand. When he took Sandy to her apartment door, he held her gently and kissed her for the first time on the mouth. "That was nice Sandy. I hope I didn't frighten you."

She looked into his liquid brown eyes and put her arms around his neck and kissed him back. "Not in the least Ramon."

"I'll call you tomorrow, Sandy."

Sandy saw her doctor the next week.

"Doctor, I have met someone I really like. Is sex out of the question for now?"

"No, not at all Sandy. You're recovering remarkably. Just don't get too rambunctious."

She laughed.

"If something hurts or doesn't feel right stop whatever you're doing. Let me know if you have any questions. Do you need some pills?"

"Yes, thank you doctor."

Ramon called Sandy and asked her if she would like to come to dinner at his house on Saturday.

"Ramon, I would love it! What can I bring?"

"Not a thing. I'm going to take the easy way out and order in. We can watch a movie at my house or do whatever you want."

"Okay."

"I'll pick you up at 7:00 o'clock."

Ramon picked Sandy up and they drove to his house.

"What did you order Ramon?"

"Chinese, is that okay?"

"I love it."

"I also have quite a few DVDs but we can do whatever you want."

The Chinese food was delicious. There were so many selections. Afterward they put on a DVD and sat on the sofa close together.

"Let's get more comfortable, you can lean back on me Sandy so your back will feel better."

She did so and Ramon put his arms around her. She could feel the heat between them.

"Ramon, I went to the doctor today."

"And."

"I told him that I had met someone I really liked."

Ramon's face fell.

"Is it anyone I know Sandy?"

"Yes, silly." she said. "He's sitting right next to me!"

Ramon's whole face lit up.

"Did he say you were okay?"

"Of course. I just wanted to ask him if it was alright, you know, if we became more intimate."

Ramon looked blank.

"You know, sex, Ramon."

"Oh, I see. What did he say?"

"He said no problem, I'm doing fine, just don't get too rambunctious."

They both laughed. Ramon kissed her teasing her mouth with his tongue. She loved it and she flicked her tongue playfully in his mouth. He had a muscular body and she could feel his erection on her body getting harder and harder. She moaned softly and he moved his hands between her legs undoing her pants. He gently slid her pants off. Ramon whispered in her ear.

"I want to make love to you Sandy."

She felt his hardness and unzipped his pants. He pulled off his pants and moved his body between her spread legs.

"Oh Ramon, I want you now."

He started penetrating her gently at first then moving in deeper very slowly.

"Sandy let me know if everything is okay."

"Yes Ramon, yes."

He started moving a little bit faster.

"Oh God, Ramon. You feel so good."

She was writhing with desire and they started moving together faster.

She cried, "Don't stop. Don't stop Ramon."

She started to come over and over and Ramon did too. They both cried out in the heat of their passion and climaxed together. They laid back exhausted on the bed and close together.

"Sandy, that was wonderful. I want you to stay overnight. Do you still feel alright?"

"Yes, Ramon, and I would love to stay with you."

"I even have a bed we can sleep in."

They both laughed.

"You know what sounds good Sandy?"

"What?"

"Let's make some popcorn with plenty of butter and salt and watch another DVD."

"Does that sound good, especially after all that exercise."

Ramon laughed.

"You stay here and I'll make it,"

"You're spoiling me, Ramon."

"I hope so."

Ramon knocked on the lieutenant's door one morning.
Stephen motioned for him to come in.

> "Lieutenant, I would like to talk to you on a
> personal matter and would like to take you to
> dinner one night after work."

Stephen looked surprised. He couldn't imagine what
Ramon wanted to talk to him about.

> "Of course, Ramon, when would you like to go?"

> "The sooner the better."

> "Well I'm free tonight if that's good for you."

They met outside in the parking lot after work and
Ramon said,

> "Lieutenant, how about a good steak and a beer at
> Dominic's?"

> "My favorite, I'm ready. Let's take two cars,
> Ramon, it's on the way home for both of us."

Dominic's Steak House was a popular place in San Pedro
and had the best steaks in town. They were able to get a
back booth and ordered a pitcher of beer, steak, onion
rings and baked potato with everything on it.

> "Okay Ramon, I'm curious. What do you want to
> talk to me about?"

> "Well lieutenant, I'm very much in love with
> Sandy and I want to marry her. I may be jumping
> the gun a little. I haven't asked her yet, but I am
> going to, soon. I have two questions for you. First,
> if she says yes it will be a small wedding, probably

184

at my parent's restaurant, La Puerta Abierta, on the patio. I would like you to be my best man."

"I'd be honored Ramon."

"Second, could you suggest a very nice restaurant where I could take her to propose?"

"I would suggest Melvin's."

"Thank you, lieutenant."

The dinner came and they ordered another pitcher of beer.

"When are you planning to go to Melvin's?"

"Tomorrow night"

"Ramon, I am so happy for the two of you."

Ramon just beamed.

"I can even wear two hats for the ceremony if Sandy needs someone to give her away Ramon."

"Thank you, lieutenant."

The lieutenant called Melvin's and spoke to the maitre'd, Peter, who he had known for years.

"Peter, this is Lieutenant McClary. My very best detective is bringing his girl to your restaurant tomorrow night for a very special occasion. Could you make sure they have a very good table with a view of the ocean and also a complimentary bottle of my favorite champagne? He will be making the reservation soon and his name is Ramon Ruiz."

"It will be my pleasure lieutenant. We will do everything to make the occasion a very special one."

"Thank you, Peter, and put the champagne on my account."

Ramon called Sandy the next morning.

"Sandy I am taking you out tonight for a very special dinner. Dress up and I'll pick you up after work at 7:00. That will give me time to run home and change."

"Ramon, I am all excited, what is the occasion?"

"It's a surprise Sandy."

Ramon made the reservation at Melvin's for 7:30. He was excited and could hardly wait. When he picked Sandy up she looked more beautiful than ever. Her dress matched the blue color of her eyes. He was knocked out. When they drove up to Melvin's and the valet took Ramon's car, Sandy was very impressed with the restaurant. Peter met them when they came in for their reservation and took them to their reserved table with a beautiful ocean view.

"Ramon this place is gorgeous."

Peter asked them if they would like to enjoy their complimentary bottle of champagne from Lieutenant McClary before or after dinner.

"Before dinner would be fine."

Peter brought a large bucket of the chilled champagne and poured them each a glass. They toasted each other and sipped the champagne slowly enjoying each other

186

and the beautiful ocean view. Sandy wanted to savor each moment.

"Ramon, what is this about?"

"Sandy, I love you so much and I want you to be my wife."

He held her hand. "Will you marry me?"

He saw tears in her eyes.

"Oh, Ramon I love you so much, too. The answer is yes, yes, yes!!"

Ramon had never been so happy. They were both so excited they had forgotten all about ordering dinner. The waiter brought their menus and left them to decide what they wanted to order. The toasted each other again and eventually looked at the menu. The dinner was superb. They ordered a Caesar salad, chateaubriand for two, baked potato with everything on it and creamed spinach. For dessert they had crème brulee. When they finally left, Ramon said,

"I hope you are staying at my house tonight."

"Of course I am Ramon."

It couldn't have been a more perfect evening.

CHAPTER 34

It was Sandy's turn to write Alecia. She wanted to tell her about Ramon and their upcoming wedding. Alecia, we are hoping that you and your son, Brian, and your parents can come to our wedding. There is plenty of room for everyone at my apartment. Alecia was a widow and had also lost her husband a couple of years ago from an infection of some kind. Please tell everyone how much I miss them and think of you all the time. Alecia wrote Sandy back immediately. She was ecstatic and said she and Brian would be coming and could hardly wait. Her parents were sorry they could not come because of work, but sent their love. Alecia said she would call her as soon as they could to make arrangements for the arrival date and time. Sandy was on cloud nine when she received Alecia's letter. She could hardly wait to tell Ramon when he came home from work.

The minute Ramon came home from work, Sandy said, "Ramon, guess what? Alecia and her son Brian will be coming for the wedding. I only wish her parents could come too, but they can't because of work."

Ramon was just as overjoyed as Sandy. He knew how close she and Alecia were growing up. Sandy told him many times how Alecia and her family saved her from going to another foster home. They considered her as one of their family. Sandy always felt like she owed them so much. Sandy got a note off to Alecia right away. "Ramon & I can hardly wait until you and Brian are here. I look a little different now, I took a bad fall, but am okay. Just wanted to tell you ahead of time in case you don't recognize me right away. I know you Alecia, so don't worry! I'm as healthy as horse, and look fine, otherwise Ramon wouldn't have asked me to marry him. See you both soon."

Love,

Sandy and Ramon.

CHAPTER 35

Donna needed to call her old friend in public administration in San Pedro, Joe Evans. She was calling to take him to a superb lunch and drinks for referring Ivan, her property manager, to her. Natalie, his secretary answered,

"Joe Evans office."

"Natalie, this is Donna Collins calling to keep a promise to Joe. Is he available?"

"Oh Donna, he will be thrilled. Hold on and I'll find him."

Joe came on the phone.

"Aha, you do keep your promises Donna. I take it Ivan worked out?"

"You can't even imagine Joe. I'm taking you to Melvin's. When would you like to go?"

"Boy, you're really going to butter me up. How about tomorrow 1:00?"

"You got it Joe. I'll make the reservation and see you there."

They both arrived at the same time and the maitre'd took them to their reserved table. Their waiter took their drink order, two very dry vodka martinis with an olive. When he brought their drinks, Joe said, "Tell me all about Ivan, Donna. Is he still scary as hell?"

"Yes, he is Joe and perfect for the job. I have hired him as my full-time property manager for all my apartment buildings. He is doing a superb job."

"Glad to hear it."

They went on and discussed all sorts of tid-bit information they had.

"Donna you may be able to help me out. We have an opening for a full-time secretary for one of our managers in my building. It's a wonderful opportunity for someone that has great secretarial skills, the government benefits are great and so is the pension plan."

"Let me check around Joe and I'll see what I can do. Does this mean this lunch is reciprocal?"

"Of course."

Before they left, Joe gave Donna the contact information she would need if she knew of someone for that position.

"Be sure and have them use my name as a referral."

Donna was talking to Stephen one night and told him about her lunch with Joe. She told Stephen about the secretarial position available and Stephen said he knew of somebody extremely well qualified. "Joe told me that if we have someone, to be sure and use his name as a referral." Stephen could hardly wait to let Sandy know about this. He had no idea how he would explain this to Donna if it worked out. Donna might still harbor bad feelings about Sandy since she and David were having an affair. It sounded like the position would be perfect for Sandy. He would wait until the time was right for his explanation to Donna.

The lieutenant couldn't get over how love does funny things to people. When Ramon came in the office, he would swear he was a different person. The bounce in his step seemed even higher than usual. Stephen wondered if he was doing anything strange himself. The lieutenant motioned for Ramon to come into his office. "Ramon, I have heard of a government position that is opening in San Pedro for a well-qualified secretary. I think Sandy would be perfect for the job. Let's take her to lunch today and I can give her the contact information. Would you call her and set something up right away?"

Ramon called Sandy and told her what the lieutenant had said. She was very excited and said she could meet them right away for lunch. They decided to meet at a nice restaurant by Sandy's apartment so she could actually walk there. They all met at 12:00 and sat in a large booth. The lieutenant told her the particulars and gave her the contact information. He told her to be sure and use Joe Evans as a referral and himself as well. The lieutenant also told Sandy that Joe had actually given the information to Donna Collins. "I am seeing Donna now on a personal level and she passed the job opening on to me."

"How does she feel about you giving the information to me lieutenant?"

"Well, I haven't told her yet, but I will."

"I don't want to harm your relationship with her in any way lieutenant. You've been so good to me."

"Don't you worry about a thing, Sandy. It will work out fine."

They had a good lunch and the lieutenant could see Sandy was anxious to get started on the position available. It would be a great opportunity for her. They all left on a good note and Ramon said he would call her when he was off work.

Stephen decided not to mention the fact that Sandy Grant was alive to Donna. At least not for right now. He wasn't sure what her reaction would be. He hoped that keeping this quiet for a little while longer wouldn't turn around later and bite him in the you know what. Especially with Donna. She always liked to know about everything going on. He decided he would wait a little bit longer. He felt like the keeper of secrets with all this information.

Sandy faxed the city manager, her resume with her referrals from Joe Evans and Lieutenant Stephen McClary. They e-mailed her immediately and asked her to come in for an interview the next day. They were so impressed and hired her immediately. She would start in two weeks. She and Ramon would be back from their honeymoon in Catalina by then. The salary and benefits were outstanding. Sandy could hardly wait to tell Ramon and Stephen.

Stephen told Donna he wanted to tell her something at dinner that night. He knew Joe Evans would fax her immediately thanking her for Sandy as their new hire. He might as well "Bite the bullet" and get it over with.

"What do you want to tell me Stephen?"

"Well you know the position Joe Evans told you about?"

"Yes."

"Ramon is going with someone now that I wanted to tell you about."

"Oh,"

"Yes, the woman who fell from the cliff by your big house miraculously survived that fall and has recovered after months and months of operations and plastic surgery in the hospital."

"I didn't know that, Stephen."

"Not many people did. We intentionally kept it quiet to keep her out of danger until we caught the person who pushed her and also to keep the media away from her while she was recovering in the hospital."

"I see."

"Well she and Ramon fell in love and are planning to get married. Sandy is able to go back to work

194

now and has outstanding secretarial and business skills and seemed perfect for the job."

"So..."

"So, I told her about the position and she applied and was hired right away."

Donna just sat there.

She finally said, "Well, I'm glad you told me Stephen."

"I knew you would understand, Donna."

"I'm not sure if I do, but I think so."

And that was the end of that conversation.

A few days later Stephen told Donna that Ramon and Sandy were planning to get married and Ramon asked him to be his best man at their wedding.

Donna was rather quiet and said to Stephen "I don't know how anyone could have survived that fall."

Donna was obviously still thinking about that fall Stephen had told her about earlier.

"Me neither. Someone was watching over her I guess."

Donna asked, "How does she look?"

"Completely different but just as beautiful as ever. You wouldn't recognize her. They had to do so much reconstruction."

Donna asked, "Where is the wedding going to be?"

"At his parent's restaurant in San Pedro, La Puerta Abierta."

He said, "Have you ever been there?"

"Yes. We had a charity luncheon there not too long ago. The restaurant was very authentic looking and quite pretty. I remember the food was excellent. We will probably have another luncheon there this year. What is Sandy like?"

"Very nice and personable. She's had a rough life. Bounced around from foster home to foster home growing up. That had to be awful. In spite of many obstacles she managed to earn her BA degree in business at night school and taking on-line classes."

"Was she ever married?"

"Yes, to a salesman she met at work and fell in love with. It was a very happy marriage for eight years until he was killed in a car accident. They lived at that time in Marina Del Rey. After he was killed she has been on her own and she decided to move to San Pedro."

"How did she meet Ramon?"

"I introduced them. I needed someone to watch over her while she was recovering in the hospital. I think they really liked each other and hit it off from the beginning."

"Do you like her?"

"Yes, I do. She is a very nice person. She's been through a lot and I think David took advantage of the situation and misled her. She was very vulnerable at the time and unfortunately he led her astray."

"I suppose I could see how that could happen especially with David."

"I'm glad you understand Donna. She has been doing some secretarial work from home for our department to help with her expenses until she was able to go back to work full time. The timing was perfect when this opening came up. She has excellent qualifications and does beautiful work."

"Joe called me." Donna said, "They were knocked out with her and couldn't thank me enough."

"Good, I'm glad to hear that. Sandy asked me who gave me the referral. I told her that you did and Joe Evans at the city had told you about it. She asked me what your reaction was. She was very concerned that you might be upset. She said she didn't want to harm our relationship in any way."

"And what did you say?"

"I told her I thought you would understand."

"Well, I suppose I'll have to go to the wedding."

Stephen put his arm around her.

"Don't worry about it Donna. I understand. If you don't want to go, you certainly don't have to."

"We'll see. I just feel kind of funny about it."

CHAPTER 36

The next evening Ramon and Sandy were enjoying a quiet evening at his home.

Ramon said, "Sandy I know women always like to be married in a church, would you feel bad if we were not married in one?"

"Where would we be married, Ramon?"

"I was thinking of the garden in my parent's restaurant and having the reception in the patio area."

"That sounds lovely, but is that okay with your parents? I know they go to a Catholic church, wouldn't they feel this is wrong?"

"No, we discussed it. I have something to tell you Sandy. When I first joined the police force, I was on duty one night with my partner. We were called out to a domestic violence fight going on and the neighbors said they heard gun shots. My partner and I were first on the scene and back -up was on the way. We could hear the woman screaming as got out of our car. We went quietly to the door and we could see him hitting her hard with something in his hand. We yelled, "POLICE, get your hands up now! He turned towards us and had something in his hand that looked like a gun and pointed it at us. I yelled, "DROP THE GUN OR I'LL SHOOT!!" He didn't and I shot him, killing him instantly. When something like that happens, it is always thoroughly investigated to determine if it could have been avoided. They ruled in favor of me. I have never forgotten this. Growing up I was raised Catholic and of course one of the commandments is "Thou shall not kill"."

"But, Ramon, it wasn't your fault."

"But I have never forgotten this Sandy, and I just don't think it is right to be married in the church. My parents understand this. We have a good friend that used to be a priest and has the proper credentials to marry us if this is okay with you."

"Of course, Ramon."

After Ramon told her his story, Sandy breathed a sigh of relief. She knew there was no way she could explain to Ramon what she had done to David. If she did, there certainly would be no marriage. She had to live with what she had done for the rest of her life and prayed she would be forgiven by a greater being at a much later time. Even though it was confirmed that the heart attack he had was what killed him and not the drug she had put in his drink, it still bothered her. She knew what she did was not right.

Ramon and Sandy decided on a small wedding of approximately thirty guests. Sandy wanted to be sure the owner and the tenants in her apartment building were included. Ramon wanted Ted and his wife Janet and a few special friends from work also. The patio was decorated beautifully in colored lights. They had three very good mariachi players that would entertain. They decided on a short honeymoon and were going to go to Catalina for a few days. Ramon asked the lieutenant if Donna would be interested in helping them plan where to stay and places to go, etc. in Catalina.

"Let me check with her Ramon."

The lieutenant decided to take Donna to one of her favorite ethnic restaurants in San Pedro to ask her. She kept bugging him,

"What is the occasion?"

"Well, you always take me out for steak and potatoes and I know you love ethnic food best, so I thought it might be nice for you for a change."

Donna loved the restaurant he took her to which had Thai food. She ate everything and said to Stephen,

"Quit picking at your food and moving it around on your plate. I'll broil a steak for you with potatoes when we get back to my place."

After dinner they drove back to her townhouse and she promised him in the car that she would make him a steak. Stephan inhaled the steak and potatoes. He was starving. They sat and enjoyed a drink afterwards in the study.

"Donna" he said, "I have to ask you something." Okay, she thought, here it comes.

"What is it Stephen?"

"Well Ramon was asking me if I would ask you something."

"Oh?"

"He and Sandy want to go to Catalina for their honeymoon for about three days. He wanted to know if you could maybe help them and suggest where to stay and what to do. They have absolutely no idea and know you are better than any tour guide over there."

Donna smiled at him.

"You know Stephen, sometimes you can be a little sneaky, but that's why I love you anyway. I guess it wouldn't kill me. How do you want to do this? Take them to dinner or what?"

"I think they would be delighted if we took them to dinner," he said.

"Why don't you set it up at work tomorrow."

"We could go to Breaker's 9 and meet them there. I love you Donna. I'll do it tomorrow."

"I think I love you more, Stephen."

On Saturday night, Donna and Stephen met Sandy and Ramon at Breaker's 9 for dinner. When Donna saw Sandy she couldn't believe how beautiful she looked.

"Sandy, you look absolutely gorgeous."

They no longer looked like each other, but each a beautiful woman, very distinctive and different.

"Stephen has told me about the upcoming
wedding. We are so excited for you and Ramon."

They went to their reserved table which had a spectacular
view of the ocean.

Stephen said, "This is one of our favorite restaurants we
hope both of you like it, too."

They ordered drinks and thoroughly enjoyed their
dinners. Donna gave them the itinerary she had made for
them on where to stay and what to do in Catalina for their
honeymoon. "You guys are going to love Catalina.
There's something to do for everyone there."

"Thank you Donna for making this itinerary for
us."

"You're welcome."

"I know Stephen is going to be Ramon's best man.
I would love to be your bridesmaid Sandy, if you
haven't selected one already."

"Oh Donna, that would be wonderful!"

Apparently, any reservations Donna had about Sandy
earlier were long forgotten.

While they were waiting for dessert, Donna and Sandy
went to the ladies' room. As they came out, Sandy was
behind Donna a few feet and someone tapped her on the
shoulder.

She turned around and a waiter said, "Hi there, nice to
see you back."

Startled, Sandy said, "Oh, I'm sorry, you must have me confused with someone else. This is my first time here."

She noticed the name tag on his shirt said Rodger.

He said, "I usually don't forget such a pretty face." Sandy just smiled and said, "Well thank you."

Donna overheard them but pretended like she hadn't. She thought that seemed kind of strange. They continued back to their table and Donna said, "You look so pretty tonight Sandy. Was that waiter trying to hit on you?"

"No, I think he was just being friendly."

Donna didn't mention the incident to anyone, but it stayed in the back of her mind. She kept thinking about it off and on. She remembered how David used to love going to Breakers 9. "Oh well," she thought, "Just forget it."

When they left, Sandy thought,

"I certainly do not need to come here again."

She didn't need any reminders of that horrible day when David surprised her at Breakers 9.

CHAPTER 37

Sandy called her marina boat manager, Jim Porter.

"Jim, this is Sandy just calling to see if you know anyone who might like to buy my boat?"

"Not really, Sandy."

"Do you know a good broker I could list it with?"

"That I do, his name is Carl. Let me give you his number."

"Thank you, Jim."

She called Carl and they made an appointment for the next day. He said he could come by her apartment since his office was close by. Carl came to her apartment and suggested a reasonable price for the boat "as is". She signed for a one month listing and told him if it didn't sell quickly she would either extend the listing or consider cancelling.

"I know a month isn't very long Carl, but I have some pressing issues that could possibly take up a lot of my time."

He agreed and started working on selling it right away. He called her within two weeks and told her he had two low ball offers but would still like to go over them with her. She agreed and he came over to her apartment that day. He brought her the two offers. The first one she said no to right away. The second one she froze when she read the prospective buyers name. It was Rodger Henderson and his occupation was listed as a server at Breaker's 9. She couldn't believe it. Sandy had heard Ramon and the lieutenant say many times they didn't believe in coincidences and neither did she.

> "Don't give up, Sandy. I will cancel both of these low ball offers, and call a few more of my prospects."

CHAPTER 38

When Sandy and Ramon met Alecia and Brian at the Los Angeles Airport (LAX) everyone was ecstatic. They were so happy to see each other and after much kissing and hugging Sandy introduced them to Ramon.

Sandy said to Brian, "You're so tall and handsome you're all grown up."

Alecia said, "Sandy, let me get a look at you. You're just as beautiful as ever. Why didn't you tell me about your fall?"

"I didn't want to worry you Alecia."

"For Pete's sake, that's what friends are for, Sandy."

"Let's get your luggage and I'll take you to my apartment so you can relax a little before dinner and change clothes."

Sandy was living with Ramon permanently at his house now so this was perfect. Ramon took everyone to dinner that night. They went to a well-known surf and turf restaurant with a great view of the ocean. Ramon wanted to show them the ocean right away. They loved it. Alecia told them during dinner that Brian had been accepted to the University of Southern California (USC) on a scholarship and would be starting in the fall. A light bulb went off in Sandy's head. She wanted to tell Ramon about her idea after they got home. She knew it wouldn't matter, he always told her yes if she really wanted something but she always liked to run things by him anyway.

After dinner, Ramon and Sandy drove Alecia and Brian to Sandy's apartment. Her lease was still in effect until the end of the month.

Sandy said, "Get a good night's sleep and we will call you about nine tomorrow since it's Saturday and Ramon and I have the day off. We'll all go to breakfast and then show you some of the sights."

When they were home at Ramon's, Sandy could hardly wait to tell Ramon about her idea. They were having an after-dinner drink in the study and Sandy said, "I have a great idea, Ramon, and I want to know what you think."

"I love all your ideas Sandy, but tell me anyway."

"Well, you know I would like to sell my boat and Alecia told me Brian is going to USC in the fall. Why not give my boat to him as a gift. His family literally saved me and I would like to do something nice for them."

"I think that's a wonderful idea Sandy. I think he'll love that boat and Alecia can help him make the boat look like a guy lives there. Do it, Sandy."

"It shall be done Ramon. I'll call Carl first thing in the morning and cancel my listing with him."

Sandy wanted to surprise Brian with the boat as soon as possible. He was at USC one day checking out where his classes would be and buying books. Sandy took advantage of him being gone most of the day and took Alecia down to show her the boat.

"Do you think he'll like it Alecia?"

"Oh Sandy, he'll be crazy about it."

"Help me take down some of these frou-frou things and we'll make it look more like a guy's boat. I'll have the name changed before he sees it to 'Brian's Getaway'."

"Oh Sandy, he's going to go crazy!"

After the name was changed, Sandy picked up Alecia and Brian one morning to go to breakfast.

Sandy said, "Let's go for a ride down by the marina after we eat."

Brian couldn't get over the number of boats in the marina. They parked the car.

Sandy said, "I want to show you something." They walked down gangway 15 to slip 4.

Brian raised his voice. "Look at that boat!! It says 'Brian's Getaway'."

"That's because its all yours, Brian."

"You've got to be kidding, Sandy."

"No, I'm not. Let's go aboard and see what you think."

Brian was in shock.

"This is just too cool."

"Now you've got a place to go when you need a break from school, Brian."

"Sandy, I love it, I bet this was your boat, wasn't it?"

"Yes, and now it's all yours and I know you'll enjoy it. I want you to meet the marina manager before we leave. The security is very good here and you should give him your contact information at school and, also, your schedule of classes. He's a good guy and he will take good care of you and your boat."

"Thank you, thank you, Sandy. On holidays I can even take boating lessons too."

"That's exactly what I did Brian. Let's go meet Jim Porter the marina manager now. I know you two will become good friends. He's anxious to meet you."

CHAPTER 39

Roberto and Beatrice closed their restaurant, "La Puerta Abierta" for Ramon and Sandy's wedding day. When the guests started to arrive, you could feel the excitement in the air. Everyone went into the beautifully decorated garden behind the restaurant's patio for the wedding itself. There were enough chairs set up for everyone. Before the wedding, Sandy talked to Alecia and Brian to prepare them for how much she and Donna looked alike before her fall. But until they actually met Donna at the wedding, they were totally shocked. The had to catch themselves during the wedding festivities from making the mistake of calling her Sandy a few times. Sandy looked gorgeous in a beautiful cream-colored lace dress just above the knee. She had an exquisite matching head piece that set everything off beautifully. Ramon was so handsome in a black tux with a dressy white shirt and tie. He looked like a movie star. The ordained minister began the wedding and everyone was silent. Ramon and Sandy repeated their vows to each other. You could tell by the way they looked at each other that they were very much in love. After they said their I do's and kissed they walked back down the aisle. Everyone clapped and cheered and they all moved to the patio which was set up for dinner. The patio was decorated with colorful lights and long dining tables were set up with chairs, emphasizing a casual and friendly atmosphere.

The dinner was served buffet style with every kind of homemade Mexican food imaginable. The mixed aromas were intoxicating. Toasts were given to the bride and groom and vice versa. The three mariachi players, close friends of Roberto and Beatrice began to perform while everyone enjoyed their dinners, but were still mesmerized by the mariachi's talent and lively sounds. They truly were a wonderful representation of their Mexican heritage and culture. After dinner and dessert, the long tables and chairs were taken out and a d-jay came in and got things jumping. But first he played a romantic song for Ramon and Sandy. They danced beautifully together and then they motioned for everyone else to join them. Then the music started to pick up and went to everything from rock to salsa, which Ramon and Sandy loved and were very good at it. The party ended late and everyone started to leave after they threw rice at the wedding couple.

Later, when Ramon and Sandy were in for the evening at Ramon's house they talked about how special their wedding was. It couldn't have been any better, they couldn't thank his parents enough. He was so glad they had their wedding in their restaurant. It seemed to make everything extra special. Sandy was so thrilled to have her closest friend Alecia there with her son Brian and also the owner and every one of the tenants in her apartment building. Ramon also had his partner Ted with his wife Janet, there and a few others who were special to him from work. They were exhausted but so happy. Ted called Ramon and Sandy a week later and asked if he and his wife Janet could stop by. They had a little wedding gift for them.

"Sure Ted, we're both here."

When they arrived and went in their house, Sandy noticed Ted was carrying a little box carefully under his arm. When he gently opened the box, the prettiest little white fluffy kitty jumped out. Sandy went crazy over her.

"Since Ramon and I work a lot," Ted said, "We thought you needed some company."

"You are so adorable!" Sandy said, "What should I call you?"

Ted said, "Sandy, remember this is a purebred Italian kitty." Emphasizing his Italian accent, he said, "Her proper name is AN GE LINA."

"What a beautiful name," Sandy said.

Angelina jumped up in Sandy's lap and started purring immediately. Ted said, "I think she knows her new home."

"Thank you both so much. What a wonderful gift from the two of you"

CHAPTER 40

When it was getting close to the time for Alecia and Brian to return home, everyone was very sad.

"Alecia, do you think your parents will be able to come with you for Christmas?"

"I know they are sure going to try, Sandy."

"We have plenty of room at our house. So we're insisting you all stay with us."

"We will have so much fun, and you can help me decorate and plan our Christmas party."

"I'll call you as soon as I know."

"I have some great Christmas decorations we can put on your boat too, Brian!"

"I can hardly wait, Sandy."

"The marina is all lit up for the holidays, Brian. Everyone decorates their boat."

"Brian," Ramon said, "be sure to call us when you return to start school."

"Before we leave for home, I would like to take all of you to an open-house one of my professors is having. I met him the other day when I was at

213

school checking out my classrooms. He's my Health and Wellness professor, Dr. Kenneth Sutherland. He seems like a real cool guy."

Alecia said, "Sure, we would like to meet him. That sounds like fun. What do you think, Sandy?"

"Absolutely. Ramon will be at work, but the three of us can go."

That Friday, the three of them went to SC to the open house. Dr. Sutherland met them at the door of his classroom and they all introduced themselves.

"Please help yourself to the coffee and pastries," he said.

Alecia and Sandy were impressed with a table of books which he had written. They all chatted comfortably since they were a little early and the only ones there. He and Alecia seemed to hit it off right away and included Sandy since she still had pain in her legs from her near fatal fall, and had some questions. As they were leaving the professor said,

"Are you all planning to be here for the Christmas holiday?"

They all said, "Yes."

Sandy said, "We will be having a Christmas party and would love for you and your wife to come."

"I would love to, but my wife and I are divorced." Then we will look forward to having you, Dr.," Sandy said.

She looked at Alecia and she knew what Sandy was thinking. When they returned to the car, Sandy said,

"Now Alecia, you definitely have to come back for the holidays. Maybe your parents can come too? We have a lot to look forward to."

When they took them to LAX to return home, everyone was teary eyed. Hugs and kisses were given and then they were gone.

Sandy said, "I can hardly wait to see them again."

"Me too," said Ramon.

CHAPTER 41

It was Sheila and Bob's tenth wedding anniversary, and Donna and Stephen decided to take their best friends to Melvin's for dinner. Stephen reserved a table but didn't ask for his special one that he usually used for business. He didn't want to run into anybody political from work. Just so they had an ocean view that would be fine. They had a large booth and ordered drinks right away. They loved just relaxing and talking about everything. Stephen lowered his voice and said,

> "The woman sitting in the booth right behind me is talking very loud."

Bob was seated across the table from Stephen and said,

> "She is being very demonstrative, waiving her arms and hands in the air carrying on about something."

All of a sudden, her hand flew up knocking her wig off her head high in the air. The wig flew in the booth behind her and right in front of Stephen. He caught it and before he knew it, she turned and snatched it out of his hand. She slapped it back on her head and turned back around to her table facing her partner without missing a beat in her conversation. Stephen was speechless and looked at everybody in shock at their table. They could hardly contain themselves from becoming hysterical!!

Donna whispered, "This one's for the books! We will be talking about this for years!"

They ordered their dinner and noticed when she and her partner got up to leave her wig looked askew and rather lopsided on her head. The couple didn't say a word to anyone as they left.

Donna said, "That was unbelievable. You would think that she would have apologized and at least gone to the ladies room to make sure she had that thing on straight."

They all started laughing again.

> "This has been an unforgettable night in more ways than one." Sheila said.

CHAPTER 42

One night, Donna and Stephen decided to stay in for dinner at her house which was unusual. They usually went out, but it was raining and Stephen built a nice fire in the fireplace in the study downstairs. Donna lit some candles and the doorbell rang with their delivery food.

"Chinese! Perfect." said Stephen.

They ate their Chinese by candlelight and soft romantic music played in the background. After dinner they moved to the sofa and started to fool around. One thing led to another and before they knew it they were in the throes of passion. The next week, Donna was having a meeting with some of her board members at her house when all of a sudden, they heard someone cry,

"Yes Stephen, oh yes Stephen!"

Donna started blushing. One of the members said, "Did you say something Donna?"

"No, I didn't, it's probably the TV. I have a friend watching the news in the other room."

They all looked at each other with a funny look on their face.

Donna said, "Will you excuse me for a minute? I'll be right back." She went into the study and said to Stephen,

> "Would you please move Henry into the back room until out meeting is over?"

> "Sure, why?"

> "Well, apparently he picked up some of the words I used when we were having so much fun the other night and made everyone aware of it."

> "What do you mean?"

Donna said, "Well, he apparently picked up on me saying in a rather excited tone "Oh yes Stephen, yes Stephen." For god's sake, he even sounded just like me. I am so embarrassed."

Stephen started cracking up.

> "It's not funny Stephen,"

and she marched out of the room to rejoin her guests. After the guests left, Donna said to Stephen,

> "From now on we will have to remember not to be within Henry's earshot when we make love, especially if we are downstairs."

Stephen laughed and said, "I bet most people don't have a bird as smart or as funny as Henry!!"

CHAPTER 43

Stephen was spending more time at Donna's than at his own place. They had talked about marriage, but after her two bad experiences she convinced Stephen to wait a bit. They loved each other and were having such a great time together she just wanted to leave it like that for the time being. It was hard for Stephen to understand because he had been happily married before. He felt that marriage completed a relationship. He loved staying over, which he did most of the time unless he had some really complex case he was working on at his office.

She told him, "I don't know Stephen, I'm so happy with the way things are now. Just the word marriage makes me nervous, probably because of my past experiences."

"Okay sweetie. I'll try to be more patient."

"Thank you, Stephen, I hope you understand."

"I'll try my best."

CHAPTER 44

Donna loved visiting her dad. There was always something going on that was entertaining. She drove by and pulled into his driveway. Maybe he would make her one of his delicious tango mango sandwiches. She opened the door because he always left it unlocked. She heard splash, splash, splash out on the patio.

"What's going on dad?"

"Well, it's been so hot so I got Murphy one of those large circular pools for kids."

Murphy was enjoying himself swimming around in a circle in his pool.

"He's become quite the athlete!!"

Her dad thought of everything.

Donna started laughing. "He loves it doesn't he?"

Her dad said, "I was hoping you would come by. How about one of your favorite sandwiches and some chips?"

"You're a mind reader."

He went into the kitchen to fix everything. Who would have thought tuna and mango would be so good together? When they sat down his phone rang.

"Want me to answer it dad?"

"No, it will go to voicemail. You'd never find it anyway."

"How come?"

"Well Murphy is so damn smart he will answer it if he beats me. I had to put it up higher on the counter so he couldn't reach it."

"How does he do it?"

"I spied on him the other day. He picked up the receiver in his mouth, lays it down on the table and puts his ear to the receiver."

"You're kidding."

"No I'm not. If he recognizes the voice he'll even talk back in his doggie talk."

"Unbelievable. Maybe you should enter him on a TV show."

"Wouldn't hurt, and I could use the extra money. You're eating all my tuna!"

"Oh, dad!"

"Next thing you know, He'll have to have a computer!"

Donna laughed. "It wouldn't surprise me one bit."

CHAPTER 45

When Ivan gave Donna his personal information to be her property manager she noticed the date of his birthday and marked it on her calendar. She sent him a funny birthday card on that day with a large bonus check enclosed. Ivan was very moved, no one had ever done this for him. He called her right away. "Thank you so much for everything, Donna."

He felt like a very lucky guy and needless to say, Donna felt very lucky herself. She didn't know what she would do without him. Ivan loved going to Curly's Café for breakfast in the morning before work and also to see Darlene. He was a big eater, especially in the morning and always ordered the "He-Man" breakfast. Pancakes, eggs, hash-browns, bacon, sausage, and of course, hot chocolate.

Darlene said, "No wonder you are such a big guy! You're a big eater."

They weren't that busy so she sat down across form him for a few minutes.

"Darlene my best friends are having a birthday party for me. Would you like to go with me?"

"When Ivan?"

"This coming weekend on Saturday."

"Sounds like fun. Where is it going to be?"

"At the beach at Crystal Point. We'll have hot dogs, and hamburgers, lots of beer, stuff like that."

"Sure, I'll go. Will we go on your bike again?"

"Of course. I'll pick you up about 6:30."

"Okay, hold on Ivan, I think your breakfast is ready."

Curly's made a great breakfast and Ivan ate every bite with gusto. He waved at Darlene when he left.

"See you Saturday."

He picked her up on Saturday and she got on his bike, reluctantly strapping on her pink helmet.

"Good girl."

Off they went in a cloud of dust. It was a beautiful night for a beach party. All of Ivan's buddies were there. There must have been twenty big Harleys there. Ivan got off his bike and helped Darlene off. He left their helmets on the handle bars.

"Ivan what in the hell is that on the back of your head?"

Ivan had a head full of curly thick black hair. "For Christ's sake, it looks like a bun on the back of your head."

"It is Darlene. It's my "man-bun". It's very popular with the guys now."

"You've got to be kidding. What will they think of next?"

"You'll get used to it. I think some of my brothers might have one, too."

"Well, just don't start putting bows and ribbons in it."

Everybody greeted them and they joined the crowd around the campfire. They all sang "Happy Birthday to Ivan". The hot dogs and hamburgers smelled and tasted wonderful. Ivan got beers for the two of them and introduced Darlene to everyone there. The party lasted late into the evening and everyone sang "Happy Birthday" to Ivan again. Before everyone left the brothers set up their next monthly meeting which was just for the guys only. They always met on a regular basis to see if anyone needed any help or was in any kind of trouble. They were a very close-knit group and you could feel the camaraderie.

When Ivan dropped Darlene off he said, "You know Darlene, I think you may be a natural for a bike."

"Say what? You've got to be kidding."

"No, really. You're catching on very fast. Think about it. I'll even pay for lessons for you."

"Let me give it some thought, Ivan. Are you thinking I should get my own bike?"

"If you think you would like one, I could help you pay for it. It's a lot cheaper than driving a car and then you wouldn't have to take a bus or walk to work. Something to think about. We could ride to some really nice places on our days off."

"Ivan, I'm going to have to think about this for a while. I hope you understand."

"I do," Ivan said.

Ivan got a call from his ex-girlfriend, Sally the day after the beach party.

"Hi Ivan, it's Sally."

"Well hi."

"It was nice to see you last night. Ivan, I wanted to let you know that Ben and I have decided to split permanently. I didn't know if you were going with the girl you were with at the party, but I just wanted to let you know that I'm available. Guess what Ivan? I have my own bike now."

"That's great Sally. Did you take lessons already?"

"You bet and I'm a whiz."

Ivan asked her again about Ben.

"Are you sure you and Ben have split?"

"Absolutely!"

The brothers were always careful not to step on each other's toes.

"Well Sally, let's go for a bike ride together. When are you available?"

"The weekends are best."

"Okay, that's good for me too. Why don't I come by Saturday around noon and we'll head out?"

"Great."

"Are you still at the same address?"

"Yes I am. See you then."

When Ivan arrived at Sally's apartment he knocked on her door.

"Hi Ivan, come on in."

"Where is your bike?" he asked.

"I keep it in the living room, I'll show you. It's the safest place to keep it around here. What do you think?"

"I love it Sally and it's definitely your color."

"It's a pretty color red isn't it? I also have a matching helmet."

Ivan took the bike outside for her and off they went. They decided on a long ride down the coast and they would stop someplace nice for lunch. It was a beautiful day to ride by the ocean. They were coming home about 5:00 pm and a bus went by them. Darlene was on the bus going home from work and spotted Ivan right away on his bike. She also noticed a bright red bike with a girl riding beside him. She could see her long blonde hair blowing in wind underneath her helmet. Darlene didn't know what to think, but maybe it was for the best. Biking wasn't her thing and she knew it.

A few days later, Ivan went to Curly's for breakfast. He liked their breakfast, and it was on his way to Donna's apartments. He didn't see any reason to not go there just because he and Darlene weren't going out at all.

227

When he walked in Darlene said, "Hi stranger, long time no see."

"I know, I've been busy."

"Would you like your same thing for breakfast?"

"You bet." Ivan said.

After he finished, Darlene said, "I'm sorry I didn't take to biking like you thought I would, Ivan."

"That's okay Darlene. It's not for everyone."

"Would you like your helmet back?"

"Okay, I'll give it to one of my biker buddies. One of their girlfriends might need one. Biking has always been a major part of my life Darlene, it's like an extension of me. I hope you understand."

"Yes, I do."

"But we can still be good friends, right?"

"Absolutely, Ivan."

Ivan and Sally were really starting to enjoy each other. They had a lot in common especially with the biking. On their days off they would take long rides, just the two of them, and stop for lunch and browse the stores wherever they were. Other times they would meet the brothers at a rendezvous spot and drink beer and have lunch and just carouse around the area with them. It was a perfect release from his busy work schedule at the apartments. Ivan thought this was probably how Donna felt when she escaped to Catalina periodically. One day after he returned home from work he had a frantic phone call from Sally.

"What's the matter Sal?"

"You won't believe it Ivan. I'm in the slammer for shoplifting."

"What on earth for?"

"I was just minding my own business at the grocery store by my apartment, and I thought I'd take in my own personal bags for a change like everyone else does nowadays. Normally I just pay extra for the bags. Well I wasn't thinking and forgot to check out and walked out the door. Just from habit I must have thought I had already checked out when I saw the bags in the basket. The manager came running outside and told me to go back in the store and come with him to his office. He called the police and told them I was shoplifting and they came and even put cuffs on me and took me to the Sheriff's Station here in town. I tried to explain, but no one was listening. Can you come down and help me?"

"I'll be there in ten minutes."

Ivan talked to the Sheriff and bailed Sally out, but she still had to appear before the judge in court at a scheduled date and time.

When Sally's court date came up, she explained everything to the judge. He seemed very understanding and tossed the case out, but still put her on probation for a year.

>"Can you believe that Ivan? Thank you so much for helping me. Is my bike okay?"

>"I put it in my apartment for safe keeping. Let's go back to my apartment and have a drink. We'll light some candles and put a hex on that store manager."

>"Good idea, Ivan."

And off they went.

>"Thank you for taking care of my bike."

>"I was glad to help, Sally."

CHAPTER 46

Stephen was involved in assisting some of his detectives in a big drug bust in San Pedro. It was taking an unusual amount of his time. He told Donna that until everything was squared away he thought he had better stay at his own house. He was on the phone all hours of the night and also working long hours in the evenings. Donna didn't realize how she was used to having him at the house until he was no longer there. She really missed him. She called him late one night just to tell him how much she missed him and that she loved him. Stephen thought that maybe the long work hours was the best thing that could have happened. He hoped so, maybe she was finally coming around.

Stephen stopped by one evening to see Donna when he had a break.

"How are things going without me?"

"Not good. I always think something is missing around here."

"Have you had dinner yet?"

"No, and I'm starved."

"Why don't you stay and I'll cook tonight."

Stephen looked surprised. He knew she never cooked.

"Stephen, what's your favorite frozen dinner?"

He started laughing.

"Well I see that nothing's changed around here. Let's order Chinese."

"That's always good."

"You know what I like about Chinese, Stephen?"

"What?"

"I love eating out of all the cartons and if we want to kick it up a notch, I have two very nice paper plates. How good does it get? No fuss before and no mess afterward. When you think about it Stephen, maybe we don't even like Chinese. Maybe it's just what we do afterwards."

"You could be right, Donna."

"Which reminds me Stephen, you better move Henry out of ear-shot. You know what happened last time we had Chinese."

"Good idea."

"We don't want him adding to his off-color vocabulary."

"I'll call in our favorite things."

Their Chinese food was wonderful and they ate almost everything. It almost seemed like old times except Stephen would have to leave for work afterwards.

"Stephen, can you tell me anything about that drug thing you're working on?"

"Not really, but we are getting closer all the time."

232

"I'm glad to hear it."

"How are your apartments?"

"Fantastic, thanks to Ivan. He's doing a super job."

CHAPTER 47

Ivan went to the brother's monthly meeting to catch up on everything. There was a rumor to watch out for a dangerous drug gang in San Pedro. Donna had mentioned to Ivan that Stephen was hard at work on a drug bust in their area. That was the major topic of conversation at the brother's meeting.

Ivan said, "If anyone sees or hears anything suspicious let me know immediately. I have a good friend, Lieutenant McClary, with the police working on it and I'll let him know. So, stay alert and keep your eyes open!"

They all agreed in unison and gave their brotherly chant in support of Ivan and his friend, the lieutenant.

One afternoon, Ivan went to see a Mr. Robins on the second floor of one of Donna's apartment buildings. Mr. Robins had called Ivan with a complaint but didn't want to discuss it on the telephone. He asked Ivan if he could stop by in the afternoon to see him personally. Ivan knocked on Mr. Robins' door.

> "Hello Mr. Robins, I'm Ivan your property manager. How can I help you?"

"Thank you, Ivan, for coming by. Please come in and sit down. Can I get you anything to drink?"

"No, thank you. Tell me what this is about Mr. Robins."

"Something is going on here that seems very suspicious. The apartment on the other side of me has people coming and going all hours of the night and into the early hours of the morning."

Mr. Robins said, "I guess there is a new tenant in there now?"

"That's right. Does that go on every night or just some nights, Mr. Robins?"

"Well, lately it seems like every night. Also, I think I heard gun shots the other night."

"Did you call the police?"

"No. The shots stopped and I thought maybe it was a car backfiring. It's always been quiet here in the evening. I just thought I should let you know."

"Mr. Robins, you did the right thing."

Ivan gave him his card with his emergency number on it.

"I want you to call me if this continues."

"I will."

"What time of the evening does this start?"

"About 8:30. Right after it gets dark and continues until three or four in the morning."

"Mr. Robins, I will look into this right away. Thank you for calling me."

"You're welcome."

Ivan called a few of his biker buddies and said he needed a stake out of one of his apartment buildings for a couple of nights. Ivan told them what the tenant was complaining about. His buddies called Ivan after the third night.

"Your tenant is right Ivan. Comings and goings all night long." Did you have a vacancy there recently?"

"Yes, and the complaints I've been getting are about the newly rented apartment on the second floor. Ten to one the new tenant could be a member of that drug gang going in and out of that apartment."

"Looks that way, Ivan. Tough, mean looking, dudes."

"Tougher than us?"

His bike buddy laughed.

"Almost Ivan, almost. It looks like they moved their drug stash from a recently condemned warehouse in a redevelopment area close by into one of your apartments. They most likely move it out when they have orders for it."

"Thanks guys."

"Anything else we can help with?"

"No, you guys did a great job. I'm going to call my lieutenant friend right away and he will take care of it."

First Ivan called Mr. Robins, the tenant back right away.

> "Mr. Robins, this is Ivan again. We are looking into this problem now. Please do not tell anyone else what you have told me. For your safety, please remain in your apartment during the timeframe of the activity you told me about. Thank you again for your cooperation, Mr. Robins. I will get back to you as soon as I have more information." Then Ivan called Donna. "Donna, I have something urgent that Stephen and you need to know about at one of your buildings."

> "Come to my place Ivan, and I'll tell Stephen to be here. How about in an hour?"

> "You got it."

Donna called Stephen right away and repeated what Ivan said.

> "I can be there in an hour."

Carlos Mendoza, the leader of the drug gang, had several locations he used to store his large supply of drugs. One location, had been a rundown warehouse in a redevelopment area that had just been closed by the city and boarded up with "no admittance" signs. It had been condemned and the city made sure it had been completely vacated. It had worked out for Carlos because one of his gang members had just rented an apartment close by so they quickly moved all of their drugs out of the condemned building and into his apartment for temporary storage. This was one of Donna's apartment buildings and fortunately a tenant reported the unusual activity to Ivan, the property manager. When Ivan met with the lieutenant and Donna at her home to alert them of the problem, he repeated his tenant's story and also what his biker buddies told him. Donna made fresh coffee for all of them and they went into her study with the coffee to discuss the situation. Ivan repeated his tenant's story and also what his biker buddies told him. "What do you think lieutenant?"

Ivan always called him lieutenant out of respect.

> "Ivan, I think you do very good detective work and if Donna wasn't so happy with you, I would like to hire you.

Donna said, "I'll pretend like I didn't hear that, Stephen."

> "You know, this smells to me like our drug connection that we have been working on. I'm going to call my team at the office now. What time frame does this happen?"

Ivan told him.

> "Now, what is the exact address of that apartment and the apartment number the tenant is talking about?"

Ivan gave it to him. "Now might be a good time to surprise them, lieutenant."

The lieutenant took his cell phone and walked into the hallway. Donna and Ivan could hear him barking orders to Ramon and Ted and the others on their team over the speaker phone in the office.

> "ON THE DOUBLE. I'll meet you over there in twenty minutes. No sirens and be sure to wear your vests and bring tear gas!! Call in

reinforcements. We don't know how many there are and surround that apartment building."

"Thank you again Ivan. I've gotta go, so will call you both as soon as I can."

And he was out the door. On his way, Stephen also had a police helicopter standing by in case they had to alert the tenants to stay in their apartments.

Stephen made it to the apartment building in 15 minutes flat, surprisingly, with no siren on. He parked his car on a side street, grabbed a vest and shot gun from his trunk and walked towards the front of the building. Ramon and his team gave him a high sign and he joined them. They were hidden behind a construction barricade across from the apartment.

"What is your assessment so far Ramon?"

"We think it's drug related like Ivan said."

"Has anyone come in or out yet?"

"Not so far, but we are ready for them when they do. We've got good protection here behind this barricade."

Around midnight a large group started to come outside the building carrying hefty duffel bags.

The police spot light was turned on them and Stephen said over his loud speaker, "THIS IS THE POLICE!! DROP YOUR GUNS AND PUT YOUR HANDS ON YOUR HEAD!!"

Gunfire erupted immediately and they shot the police spotlight out.

Stephen yelled, "BOX THEM IN, KEEP SHOOTING!!"

The police team made a semicircle around them to contain them, guns blazing. Some of their drug members were hit and went down. Stephen said again over the loud speaker,

> "WE HAVE YOU SURROUNDED. DROP YOUR WEAPONS AND PUT YOUR HANDS ON YOUR HEAD!!"

They had no intention of surrendering and started shooting again.

Stephen contacted the helicopter, "GO! GO!"

As instructed, the helicopter circled the building repeatedly with its loudspeakers booming

> "THIS IS THE POLICE! FOR YOUR SAFETY, REMAIN IN YOUR APARTMENT. DO NOT OPEN YOUR DOOR FOR ANY REASON!!"

> "If you can take any good shots, do it," Stephen said to the helicopter pilot. "Just don't get within their firing range. LET'S NAIL THESE SUCKERS!!"

The volley of shots started to subside as more of the drug members were shot down.

Stephen said, "Let's start rounding them up guys. Ramon and Ted, get a team inside the building there's probably more in there, especially in apartment 2B. Take tear gas and masks in with you and be sure to wear your vests!"

Ramon and Ted and several others went inside the building. Everything was still. They crept up to the second floor. When they got to 2B they said,

"THIS IS THE POLICE. OPEN UP, DROP YOUR WEAPONS AND COME OUT WITH YOUR HANDS ON YOUR HEAD!"

They stood way off to the side of the door.

"BOOM!!"

A shotgun blast cut through the door knocking it off its hinges. The detectives put on their gas masks and Ramon threw a can of tear gas inside the room. They stood back, waiting. There was a lot of coughing and wheezing and then they started to stagger out.

Ramon said, "Cuff them and take them outside."

Stephen said, when everyone was outside the building, "Is everyone okay and accounted for?"

"Looks good." Ramon said.

Stephen said, "Take the ones that are still breathing and book them. Be sure and read them their rights. How many do we have?"

"Eighteen." Ramon said, "And seven of theirs are dead. Not a bad night's work lieutenant. None of our guys were hit."

Stephen called the tenant Dick Robins who had reported the problem to the management.

241

"This is Lieutenant McClary of the LAPD police department. Is everything okay up there?"

"I think so lieutenant."

"Thank you, Mr. Robins for alerting us. Everything is under control, but please remain in your apartment for the rest of the night. It will take hours to clean up this mess inside and outside."

"I will lieutenant and thanks again."

The helicopter kept circling the building announcing over the loud speaker.

"EVERYTHING IS UNDER CONTROL. FOR YOUR SAFETY, PLEASE REMAIN IN YOUR APARTMENTS FOR THE NIGHT WHILE WE REMOVE THE DEBRIS."

The duffel bags were large and heavy and carried large amounts of drugs, primarily heroin and cocaine. They were all taken to the police station and secured in the evidence room. Hours later, when everyone had returned to the station, Stephen thanked them profusely for doing an outstanding job.

"How many fatalities again Ramon?"

Ramon said, "Zero for us, seven of theirs. We incarcerated 18."

The lieutenant said, "We were lucky none of our guys were hit with all that crossfire. Those construction barricades gave us the perfect cover we needed. Everyone go home and try to get some rest. It was a good night's work. Thank you again."

Ramon said to the lieutenant, "It looks like that apartment was getting too full, so they had to move some of their merchandise to another location to fulfill order requests. Worked out perfectly for us."

Stephen called Ivan to thank him and also his biker buddies for their assistance in capturing the drug dealers. He reminded him again if he ever got tired of managing apartments, he could come to work for him.

> "But for God's sake don't tell Donna. She would kill me Ivan, she thinks the world of you."

> "Okay lieutenant. I'm just glad to help out in any way I can."

Stephen then called the tenant Dick Robins to thank him, again.

> "Mr. Robins, this is Lieutenant McClary, again from the LAPD. Thank you again for alerting your property manager Ivan, about your problem next door."

> "You're welcome lieutenant."

> "Any more problems, call Ivan or myself. Thank you again Mr. Robins."

> "You're welcome."

The lieutenant called Ramon into his office.

> "Ramon, after our guests have been processed and have gotten comfortable in their new surroundings, find me their "weakest link" and we'll interrogate him together. We need to find out

243

who their leader is and if he is with us or out in the wild blue yonder somewhere."

"Will do lieutenant."

After forty-eight hours went by.

Ramon told the lieutenant, "I think I've got our guy."

"Bring him into the interrogation room, Ramon, and we'll get started on him. What's his name?"

"Carlos Mendoza."

"Does he speak and understand English?"

"More than he lets on lieutenant."

The lieutenant came into interrogation and saw Ramon and Carlos waiting for him. Carlos was shackled to his chair.

The lieutenant introduced himself.

"Nice of you to join us, Carlos."

Carlos gave a smirk.

"Carlos, we have some questions for you. If you give truthful answers we may be able to reduce your sentence considerably. Comprende, Carlos?"

Carlos smirked again.

"Carlos are these all of your drug dealing buddies or are there others out there?"

Ramon repeated the question in Spanish to him.

"Yes, I think that is all."

"Are you all from this country?"

"Si."

"What is the name of your leader?"

Carlos shrugged.

"Is he with the others here?"

Carlos said, "No comprende."

Ramon translated in Spanish.

> "Ramon, tell Carlos that if he can tell us his leader's name and where he is we can promise him a new life here in the United States, otherwise he can spend the rest of his life in a maximum-security cell."

Carlos shrugged his shoulders.

> "Ramon, put Carlos in solitary confinement so his buddies will wonder what is happening to him. Tell him when he is ready to help us to let us know."

After a week in solitary confinement Carlos told the guard he wanted to talk to Ramon. When Ramon came to the outside of his cell they spoke in Spanish. Carlos told him he wanted to know more about the program the lieutenant mentioned.

> "I'll speak to the lieutenant and I'll get back to you Carlos."

Ramon told the lieutenant and they decided to meet with Carlos the next day. Ramon got back to Carlos later in the day. "The lieutenant would like to talk to you tomorrow." Ramon warned Carlos that if this was a waste of the lieutenant's time, they would put him back with his buddies right away. "I don't think they would be too happy to see you Carlos. They will wonder how much you have told us."

The next day Carlos was led back into the interrogation room. The lieutenant and Ramon were waiting. Ramon asked him if he would like some coffee.

"Si, café negro por favor."

Ramon brought in some black coffee for him. The lieutenant then went into detail about the witness protection program with Ramon translating. He asked if Carlos had any family.

"No."

"Bueno." Ramon said.

Ramon continued in Spanish with whatever the lieutenant said.

> "Your appearance will be changed so no one will recognize you, Carlos. You will be sent far away to live in another state in this country. You will have a comfortable place to live, some money to live on and will be given a job. Life will be good. You will, literally, become another person with a whole new life. Any questions?"

Carlos said no and shook his head.

Ramon told him, "You are being given a second chance Carlos."

The lieutenant said, "Now Carlos, we can proceed if you answer my questions I asked before."

Carlos told the lieutenant what he wanted to hear.

"First, what is your leader's name?"

Carlos said, "Jose Rivera."

"Second, where can we find him?"

Carlos gave the lieutenant the exact location of Jose's headquarters.

Ramon said, "Mucho gracias, Carlos."

The lieutenant's and Ramon's adrenaline shot up. They now knew who their leader was and where they could find him. They would go after him.

"We will check this out and get back to you Carlos within twenty-four hours. Thank you again for your cooperation."

Carlos was escorted back to solitary. When Ramon entered the name "Jose Rivera" into the police computer, he couldn't believe the lengthy list of crimes that were spewed out. It was unbelievable.

"Lieutenant take a look at this!"

"Good grief." the lieutenant said, "This guy is wanted for everything. Ramon, take Ted with you and check out the location he gave us right now. Get back to me as soon as you can."

"We're on it, lieutenant."

"If the location looks good, we will arrest him and get Carlos ready for Witness Protection."

247

"Yes sir."

When Carlos returned to his cell, he thought so far everything seemed to be going just as he had planned. The police would be after a big-time rival drug dealer, and eventually, Carlos would be able to add the members of Jose's team to his own team that had not been incarcerated. Carlos had put a lot of thought and planning into this after he and his gang was captured. If he went into Witness Protection, he could make his escape later, return to California and then make Jose's team his own. He was betting the authorities would capture Jose and incarcerate him soon with the information he gave them. He just had to be sure they captured Jose before he started recruiting Jose's team. Ramon and Ted did a stake out on the location for Jose that Carlos had given them. Everything looked good and they were confident they would be able to surprise and capture him. They went back to the station to report their findings to the lieutenant. Ramon knocked on the lieutenant's door when they returned. He waved them in and he and Ted said, they thought a surprise capture would work. Everyone was elated and ready to go. The capture went even easier than they expected. They took Jose by surprise and arrested him as he was going to his car late one night in his office buildings subterranean garage. He looked like any business executive, well-groomed and in an expensive three-piece suit. He certainly did not look like a drug dealer. They arrested him when he started to get into his late model BMW, read him his rights, and took him to the station to be processed.

Carlos wanted to know when would the Witness Protection Program start.

Ramon said, "Right away. You will be taken from prison to a safe house late tonight. Be ready about midnight."

Carlos smiled. Little did they know, they had just provided him with his escape route. They came to remove Carlos from his cell at 1:00am. He was starting to get worried and thought maybe they were on to him. He got into a police SUV, the gate opened, and out they went. Unbeknownst to the lieutenant and Ramon. Carlos was actually the leader of the drug gang they had incarcerated. He was a fairly well-educated man and had read about this "protection" program. So far it was working beautifully. He had given them the name of a big-time drug leader, Jose Rivera and his exact address. He hoped that they caught him soon. That would make his job and life a lot easier. He had given this scenario a lot of thought and planning. He would go through with it almost to the end. He would wait until after they changed his appearance and given him a new identity in Witness Protection. When they sent him to a new state he would pretend he was unhappy there and wanted to be moved someplace else. He would have all kinds of excuses to complain about. When the time was right, he would make his move and return back to California.

When they had reached his new destination, they gave him a small amount of spending money each week. He accumulated it religiously. It was enough to get him back to California. He was looking forward to being back in business. They hadn't captured all of his men and he could continue with his plan and start recruiting members from the rival gang as soon as he could when he reached California. When the time was right, Carlos would then change his identity again, dye his hair, add or lose a few pounds, maybe add glasses, get a new ID and no one would recognize him. La Dolce Vida!

When authorities in the witness protection program realized that Carlos was missing they put out a major alert to try and find him. Unfortunately, no luck. They notified Lieutenant McClary in California and told him the bad news. The lieutenant called his staff in for an emergency meeting and brought them up to date. The lieutenant then realized Carlos had tricked them and the gang leader they were after, Jose Rivera, was not the leader of the drug members they had incarcerated but another high-level drug dealer. Ramon felt terrible about his mistake. Their actual leader was Carlos.

The lieutenant said, "It was not your fault Ramon, Carlos was on to our plan all the time from beginning to end. Let's not give up on the seventeen gang members we have incarcerated. Someone might break and give us some other vital information which could be very helpful to us, so all is not lost. Actually Ramon, you are a hit with our narcotics department for nailing Jose Rivera. He's a big fish!!"

Ramon had a big smile on his face.

> "You know Ramon, it's an ongoing process isn't it? We cut the head off one and another one rears up his ugly head and takes his place. I guess all we can do is try and stay ahead of their game. The important thing is we never give up!"

The first thing Carlos did after he went missing was to buy a burner cell phone. He alerted his drug gang members in California that had not been incarcerated, that he had escaped from Witness Protection and was on his way back to California. He would be there in a few days and business would begin as usual. He told them his appearance had been changed but other than that he was the same.

Carlos always had a principal contact in charge at their key location who was available 24/7 for them on his burner phone. He called him immediately and told him the whole story.

When Carlos arrived in California, he met with the members of his gang immediately. He told them what had he had done. He went over the plan he had developed so they could start recruiting members of Jose Rivera's drug gang. Carlos had recently heard on the news that the police had captured a major gang leader, Jose Rivera. What a break. He couldn't believe they had caught him already.

Carlos said, "We can start recruiting now. Let's put out a rumor on the streets, concentrating on our rivals' area, that we are recruiting new members. A bonus is given if they are qualified and accepted. Give them our hot line 24/7 number. While Jose is incarcerated his team will soon become our team."

The lieutenant was not one to be defeated. "Ramon, let's get a hold of narcotics and see if we can beat Carlos at his own game." Ramon left a message for the narcotics "hot" undercover guy who went by the name of Eduardo Escobar. Eduardo returned the call and Ramon asked if he could meet with him and the lieutenant as soon as he could.

"What is this about Ramon?"

"It's something related to drug trafficking that you might be interested in doing as an undercover agent."

"Okay, how about 5:00 pm today?"

Ramon confirmed with the lieutenant and they set it up. When Eduardo walked in the lieutenant's office at 5:00 pm the lieutenant and Ramon thought he certainly looked the part. His thick black hair was dirty and long and tied back in a pony tail. He had a 5 o'clock shadow and his clothes were wrinkled and dirty masking his rugged good looks. He was very muscular and mean looking with tats covering his neck and arms and a few other piercings.

"Hi guys, I'm curious, let's hear it."

The lieutenant and Ramon went into detail about the capture of Carlos Mendoza and seventeen of his members. How Carlos had tricked them into turning their attention to a big-time gang leader, Jose Rivera, who they thought was the leader of the men they had just captured. For giving them this information Carlos was released into the Witness Protection Program. Carlos has recently escaped from Witness Protection and is now back in California. We are hearing that Carlos is recruiting members from Jose's team to add to his existing base.

Eduardo said, "How are they recruiting?"

"Carlos has his men infiltrate Jose's territory and is passing out a 24/7 number to call if interested. If they are qualified they will get a bonus for joining."

"What do you think Eduardo?"

"Interesting. I guess my job will be to join the gang and pass Carlos back to you and, also, their current locations, is that correct?"

"You got it Eduardo."

"I'd like to give it a try."

"How soon do I start?"

"Right away. We already checked with your superiors for approval ahead of time and you have the go ahead if you agree."

"Here is a map of the best area in San Pedro to establish contact and also the name of a cheap but clean motel in San Pedro. We already reserved a room for you. The desk clerk will have your key. Good hunting Eduardo. We don't have to tell you to watch your back at all times."

They established how they should stay in contact on a weekly basis and an emergency plan if Eduardo was in trouble or needed help.

Eduardo said, "I'm ready to go, I have a fake ID and my past history is already in the system, lieutenant, with a long history of criminal activity. Everything will look kosher whenever they check it."

Eduardo started to infiltrate the area marked on the map given to him by Ramon. He started with some of the run-down bars closest to the harbor. It didn't take long before he met someone who could tell him where he could get a joint, maybe deal a little and so on. One night someone passed a 24/7 number to him across the bar. He had a burner phone and made the call later in the night and gave them his qualifications when asked. They asked him to call back the same time the next night. He did as he was told.

> "We like your qualifications and would like to talk to you more."

> "Okay, when?"

> "Tomorrow at 10:00 pm."

They gave him an address down by the harbor then hung up.

The next night Eduardo went to the address at 10:00 pm sharp. It was almost 10:30 and he was getting impatient. It was getting foggier and he started to leave when someone came up behind him and tapped him on the shoulder.

The guy said, "Follow me."

They walked a block down the street and into a run-down warehouse. It was dimly lit inside but he saw a light on upstairs. He could see two thugs sitting by the wall watching TV downstairs.

> "Follow me upstairs."

He patted him down first and checked him for a wire. When they reached the top of the stairs Eduardo saw a man behind a desk that resembled Carlos from the picture the lieutenant had shown him, after Carlos had his new cosmetic surgery in Witness Protection.

He didn't introduce himself but said, "Sit down and tell me about yourself and what you've been doing for the last few months."

Eduardo did so, then Carlos asked, "Where are you staying now?"

"At a cheap motel in San Pedro."

"How did you hear about us?"

"I was at a local bar and someone gave me a number to call."

"How long do you intend to do this?"

"I would like it to be permanent and move up when I prove myself indispensable to you."

Carlos laughed, "I like your attitude. I'll give you a try. I'm going to put you on a probationary period for now."

"For how long?"

"Two months."

"That long?"

"What about the bonus?"

"After the two months."

"How much will the bonus be?"

"We'll see."

"Can you give me an idea?"

"Five hundred maybe more depending on how well you do."

"When do I start?"

"Right away. Give me a number where I can reach you."

Eduardo gave him his burner number. The same guy who met him came in and led him out.

When he was outside, he said to the guy, "That's it?"

"He'll call," he said and walked away.

Eduardo walked quickly back to his car. He had left his gun in his car because he knew they would search him. It wasn't safe to walk in this neighborhood for very long without some kind of protection.

The first few weeks Carlos had assigned Eduardo to menial tasks. Accompanying his men to pick up money extorted from various businesses. As they began to recruit more of the rival gang members, Carlos needed someone to help him and he decided to go with Eduardo. Carlos called Eduardo to his office.

"Eduardo, I have a new position for you."

"Does this mean I've earned my bonus?"

Carlos slapped three Benjamins on his desk.

"We'll start with this and see how well you do."

Eduardo put the bills in his pocket.

"First, I want you to start talking to the new members we have recruited. But before you do this, I want you to clean yourself up. Not only personally but the way you dress. For Christ's sake you look like some goddamn drug dealer. I don't want to have to bail your ass out of jail. After all, we are businessmen."

"Okay, what do you want me to talk to our new members about?"

"This is what I need. Find out what their organizational structure looked like. Where the businesses are located they extorted money from and their contacts there. What percentage do they take? What is their weekly/monthly income? What are their expenses? What are their expansion plans? What are their strong and weak points? Do they have any other rival dealers and are they strong or weak? That will do for starters Eduardo. Let's meet next week, same time, and you can tell me what you have so far."

Eduardo's Weekly Progress Report to Lieutenant McClary read,

"Carlos seems to have taken me into his confidence. I have more responsibility now and even have to look and dress better. Heard you have the big time gang leader Jose Rivera in custody. If he is released for any reason let me know immediately. More later, E."

The next week came quickly and Eduardo thought he was ready for Carlos.

When they met again, Eduardo asked, "I hope you are pleased with my appearance."

"Believe me, I would let you know if I wasn't."

"Carlos, here is a copy of their organizational structure. I have indicated which key men are in charge of each function."

"Good, good. Next, what are their expansion plans?"

"They are mainly in California. They plan to work their way into Wilmington and the poorer sections of Long Beach. I have marked these areas on a map for you."

"Good, very good."

"Their rival gangs include us of course, and a few other startups we could go after. Here is a list of their weak points. They need more qualified members. Their income needs to improve and their expenses decline. No surprise there."

Carlos looked pleased and slapped a few more Benjamins on his desk for Eduardo.

"What else can I do for you Carlos?"

"Well we need to give our new recruits and maybe our existing members more incentives to help us get larger. Find out how our member's cut compares to Jose's. Did they have perks at all?

Let's meet again at the end of the week. I'll call you"

"You got it boss."

The meeting was over.

They met again at the end of the week as planned.

"Their cut is the same as our Carlos."

"They have no perks at all."

"Okay, let me think about the perks." Carlos said.

"To improve their income, I have indicated on this map for you the businesses that they extort money from. The ones where the take is way too low and needs to be increased are marked for you," Eduardo said.

"Yes, that is good." Carlos said.

"To reduce expenses, we need the same teams to cover businesses that are close together which would reduce their wasted time and expenses going from place to place."

"I like it Eduardo, I like it. You keep this up and I'm going to have to put you on salary. How does that sound?"

"Very good, Carlos. I can use it. What is next?"

"I want you to find us a few new locations. As they say, it's not good to keep "all your eggs in one basket." We need to spread out more."

"How many locations do you want?"

"Let's start with three."

"How large do you want each location?"

"About 1,000 square feet. Take a week or so and get back to me."

"Will do."

"I will use one of the locations for my headquarters. I don't like this location."

Eduardo's latest message to the lieutenant read, "I am helping to increase his business and am now looking for three new locations for him. All is well. E"

Carlos told Eduardo to stick to warehouses for the locations, but not in redevelopment areas.

"Why is that Carlos?"

"I'll tell you when I have a little more free time. Just make sure they are not in any redevelopment areas."

"All right."

Eduardo came up with two more locations within a couple of weeks. He was working on the third when Carlos called him in. Carlos seemed pleased to see Eduardo.

"Eduardo I want to take you to dinner tonight if you are free. An old friend of mine owns a place and owes me a favor. I have a surprise for you."

"Sure Carlos, where and what time?"

Carlos told him and they met at his friend's Italian restaurant at 8:00 pm. It was well known for its superb food and fine wine. Carlos was sitting in a back booth reserved for him and his guests to give them plenty of privacy from the customers. He was seated with his back to the wall facing the door. The maître'd took Eduardo to the reserved booth for Carlos. Eduardo was curious about the surprise Carlos had for him. The wine started flowing freely with some special appetizers the owner had for Carlos and his guest.

"Eduardo I am putting you on salary as of today."

When he said the amount, Eduardo tried not to look surprised. It was very generous.

"Thank you, Carlos."

"You earned it Eduardo. I think we are okay for now with the two new locations you have come up with. I will be moving into the last one right away. Eduardo, I could really use some help with the interviews for the new recruits. How does that sound?"

"Sounds good."

"Also, I think we can recruit a few of the smaller groups you mentioned earlier."

"Will do, Carlos. I'll start right away."

Eduardo was thinking he was glad he had a photo of the new gang leader that was presently incarcerated. He could just see him being released for some crazy reason and answering their 24/7 hotline message for a position.

"Oh, I wanted to tell you Eduardo, why I prefer warehouses, but not in a redevelopment area. The last location we had was in a redevelopment area. They city condemned it without any warning and boarded up the building. We had to move our merchandise immediately. It wasn't a problem because one of our members had just rented an apartment close by. He made a deal with the building owner that we could move our merchandise in his apartment right away, but only for a limited time. The owner seemed like a savvy guy, his name was David something or other, Conners or Collins. He let on like he was the owner but, apparently, he no longer was. He sensed we were under pressure from the city so he asked for a pretty good cut for letting us stash our goods. We agreed at that time to pay him. We were able to move everything in okay, but it became a problem when we started taking the goods out at all hours. A tenant complained and that's when they arrested us. I also lost some of my men in a shoot-out with the police."

Eduardo's next weekly progress report read:

"On salary now. Picked up two new locations for them. Found out the ex-owner of the apartment building where you captured them is a David Conners or Collins. He was on the take and he let them store their drugs in a vacant apartment he had temporarily. Whatever happened to him?

"E"

The lieutenant and Ramon did not know about this incident with David but they knew he needed money badly after his divorce from Donna. His death seemed to be making more and more sense all the time. If the heart attack hadn't killed him, the drug gang might have since he took advantage of their situation and charged them so much to store their drugs.

Of all the gangs Eduardo had infiltrated, he found himself liking Carlos much more than any of the other dealers, but he knew from experience not to let his guard down. The man could change very quickly and become extremely dangerous. He didn't get where he was by being a nice guy. Eduardo wisely remembered the advice, "Be sure to watch your back." Eduardo was actually enjoying the interviews with the new recruits.

Carlos said, "I like seeing our membership beginning to expand so quickly. You know Eduardo, at the rate we are growing, we might move into the cartel market in the not so distant future. We couldn't be more ideally located than we are. Right smack in the middle of the two largest harbors in the nation."

"You're right Carlos."

The next Weekly Progress Report read:

> Have been interviewing new recruits for Carlos. Expansion moving right along. Carlos has his mind set on the cartel market if we keep growing as fast as we have.

E

The recruiting effort had a domino effect. The recruiters started telling friends of theirs and they would call the 24/7 line and so on. Carlos was amazed. He was beside himself and grinning from ear to ear. It wasn't long before his drug business was growing into a little empire. Carlos noticed how quickly Eduardo qualified possible recruits over the phone. He didn't waste any time.

In the next Weekly Progress Report. Eduardo gave the lieutenant the exact information he was looking for. He gave the exact locations of the two warehouses and marked the one where Carlos had his office. Everyone at the station was elated. This was the key takedown information they needed. Expect Next Progress Report in two days.

E

Last Weekly Progress Report read, "Happy Birthday"

"E."

The last progress report contained their signal and code to pick Eduardo up the next day at 10:00 am at their prearranged location and bring him in.

Alberto, one of Carlos' top men knocked on his office door the day of the last progress report.

"Come in, what is it?"

264

Alberto sat down across from Carlos and slid a piece of paper across his desk to him. Carlos picked it up and read it.

> "What the hell is this Alberto?"

> "I stopped in a drug store on the other side of town last night when Eduardo came in. He was leafing through the magazines and didn't see me. I saw him put a piece of paper into one of the magazines and then he left. I was curious so I took out the piece of paper from the magazine."

He nodded toward the piece of paper across from Carlos.

> "Very interesting, Alberto. I don't know what it means, but keep an eye on him. Don't let him out of your sight!"

That next day Eduardo left to eat an early breakfast before driving to their pick-up spot. When he was in the restaurant, a feeling of uneasiness came over him. Carlos would usually text him while he was eating breakfast just to let him know if he had anything for him that day. De nada. Eduardo had a very uneasy feeling after eating and left the restaurant and got in his car to drive to meet his contact at their pre-designated pick-up location. Just as a precaution he checked his gun, the magazine and the action. Good to go. He laid it on the passenger side of the seat close to him.

As he drove, he kept looking in his rear view and side mirrors for a tail. He thought he spotted the same car a couple of times, but he wasn't sure. Eduardo punched the

hot line emergency number for Lieutenant McClary.
Ramon answered.

"Ramon, did you get my "Happy Birthday" message?"

"No we did not Eduardo."

"They're on to me then. I am on my way to our pick-up spot now. I thought I spotted a tail but wasn't sure."

"We're on our way, Eduardo."

"Step on it Ramon."

"You got it."

When Eduardo reached his destination, he parked the car to wait for Ramon. A few minutes later, he spotted the car he thought was tailing him park around the corner. He could see the front of the car sticking out. It looked like there were two men in the front seat. Eduardo removed the safety on his gun and also stuck a reserve magazine in his jacket. The two men got out of the car and Eduardo recognized them as two of Carlos' gang members. They started walking towards his car. He could spot a gun each one had at his side. Eduardo started his car and stepped on the engine driving erratically towards them. He knew a moving target would be harder to hit. One of the men took aim, fired, and hit his window but missed him. Eduardo shot him and he went down. He saw the other start to take aim and Eduardo hit the side of him with his car before he could fire. He hoped they had not had the time to alert any of the other gang members.

Eduardo finally heard police sirens and saw flashing lights. Three police cars pulled up and stopped.

He heard over the loud speaker, "COME OUT WITH YOUR HANDS UP!"

Eduardo did as he was told and saw Ramon and waved.

He heard Ramon say to the others, "It's okay guys stand down. He's one of ours."

Eduardo was never so glad in his life to see anyone. He got in the police car with Ramon.

> "Welcome home Eduardo. Good to have you back."

Ramon told the other two police cars that came with him as back-up to stay and follow up on the proper procedure for the crime scene. He and Eduardo were going back to the station as soon as they gave them the information they needed for their report.

Ramon called the lieutenant on his cell phone.

> "We've got Eduardo, safe and sound and are on our way back to the station."

> "Ramon, put Eduardo on the line."

> "Hi lieutenant."

> "Good to have you back Eduardo."

> "Thanks lieutenant. Now is a good time to surprise Carlos, lieutenant. Apparently the two members I just wasted that were following me did not have time to notify Carlos. No one else came

after me. Now would be a good time to catch them off their guard."

"Good advice, Eduardo. We're on it."

When Ramon arrived back at the station with Eduardo there was just a small staff there on call. Ramon buzzed the lieutenant.

"Hi Ramon."

He could hear the excitement in the lieutenant's voice.

"Tell Eduardo that we have Carlos and his men surrounded at the locations he gave us. See you guys as soon as we have everything under control and ready to bring them in. Gotta run for now."

Eduardo was anxious to see if Carlos was among the captured. He would wait for the lieutenant's return. To kill some time, he went to see his narcotics superior and let him know he was back.

A couple of hours later, he heard a lot of commotion in the station. The lieutenant was back and went upstairs in search of Eduardo to tell him "Mission Accomplished." When Eduardo saw the lieutenant in the hallway, he had a big grin on his face for Eduardo which told him they had been very successful.

"How many lieutenant?"

"Twenty-five."

"Any casualties?"

"Nope, zero for us, a few of them wounded, but no casualties."

"It won't take long for them to be fingerprinted and have photos taken. Then we will know if we have Carlos. Let's get some coffee."

They didn't have to wait that long before they buzzed the lieutenant.

"Come on down, lieutenant."

"Let's go Eduardo."

As they entered the ID department, everyone shouted.

"We've got him for you, lieutenant."

The lieutenant patted Eduardo on the back.

"Thanks to this guy."

Eduardo also identified Carlos from his picture.

Eduardo said, "Outstanding lieutenant, you got him!" Then he also pointed to another photo.

"Lieutenant, you have another bonus. I recognize this guy and I'm pretty sure he is their drug carrier, 'The Mule'. He came into a restaurant one night when I was there with Carlos and I overheard some of their conversation."

"We can't thank you enough, Eduardo." Said the lieutenant.

"I want you to go home now and get some rest, you deserve it! Come see me before you go back to narcotics. I'm sure they missed you. Before I forget, I better notify Witness Protection that we

269

have Carlos in custody. They will be happy to call off their search.

Stephen called Donna right away.

"Big celebration tonight, honey, let's go to my favorite steak house, Dominic's."

"What's the occasion, Stephen?"

"I'm patting myself on the back and celebrating."

"What happened?"

"We have wrapped up our drug bust and it's out of commission."

"That's wonderful Stephen!"

When they arrived at Dominic's they ordered their favorite drinks right away, two very dry vodka martinis with olives.

When the drinks came, Donna said, "This calls for a very special toast to you Stephen. Congratulations."

They raised their glasses and toasted each other.

When they came home after dinner Stephen said,

"I'm beat Donna, I think I'll call it a night and turn in pretty soon."

"I'll join you in a few minutes honey, I have to make a couple of phone calls."

CHAPTER 48

The following week was filled with two very special events. The first event was a public ceremony held at the City Hall in San Pedro. Since the drug ring was centralized and captured in San Pedro, this was the perfect place to honor the LAPD police department and those individual citizens who contributed to their capture. You could feel the excitement in the air as you walked in the building. There was plenty of seating available. The podium was on a large raised platform which, also, had seating on each side of it for the honorees and the officials in attendance. The first few rows below the podium were reserved for the honorees' family members and close friends. The audience was packed with the residents from San Pedro and Palos Verdes. Sandy had even spotted Bob Griffith and the tenants in her apartment building earlier. She was also surprised to see Charlie, the bartender, and Jim Porter from the marina.

Since San Pedro was a community and not a city, they had an honorary mayor who was the introductory speaker at the event.

The mayor said, "Before we begin, I would like to introduce the local city officials that are here with us

271

today, and our special guests Elliot Harper, the Los Angeles District Attorney, Dr. Josh Ryan, the Medical Examiner of Los Angeles and Joe Evans, our Public Administrator of San Pedro."

Josh said in a low voice to Elliot,

"Is Sandy here yet, Elliott? Where is she?"

"She's the first one in the first row, Josh."

"Oh my god. She is absolutely beautiful."

Elliott saw Josh's eyes start to fill with tears.

"I can't get over it. I am so glad I was able to come today. I can hardly wait to tell my staff. They will be just as excited as I am. They ask about her all the time."

Elliott said, "She and Ramon Ruiz, one of the policemen being honored, were just recently married."

"What a lovely story." Josh said.

"I think she is scheduled to sing our national anthem, Josh."

Next, the mayor said please stand for the Pledge of Allegiance to the Flag. The mayor then introduced Mrs. Sandy Ruiz and said, Sandy will lead us in our National Anthem. Ramon escorted her up the steps to the podium. She sang beautifully with the audience enthusiastically joining her. Sandy's voice was absolutely incredible. When she finished, everyone was so moved that there wasn't a dry eye in the house. Ramon escorted Sandy back down the steps to her seat in the front row. She was seated next to his parents, Beatrice and Roberto Ruiz. The crowd gave a standing ovation and couldn't stop cheering and clapping to show her their appreciation.

The mayor said, "Thank you Sandy, you sang that beautifully."

The mayor began, "We are here today to honor our outstanding LAPD police department and those special citizens who have made our city safe and free from drug violence. Their extraordinary bravery and courage was incredible. To my left is Lieutenant Stephen McClary of the LAPD, who led the capture of the dangerous drug ring."

The crowd broke out in loud applause and cheering.

The lieutenant stood and said, "Thank you. I would now like to introduce you to Ramon Ruiz and Ted Sicilliano, two of our departments finest."

The crowd went wild again. The lieutenant praised them over and over again for the detective's heroism.

The lieutenant said, "Next, I would like to introduce some of our private citizens who were so instrumental in this capture. Ivan, please stand and introduce your biker brothers."

Ivan did so, and each one of them stood when they were called.

"This is Tyrone, Jake, Curly, and Tiny."

They stood with their helmets held high in the air and chanted in unison. The crowd broke into more yelling and cheering in support. The rest of the biker brothers in the second row also stood and raised their helmets and chanted. Everyone was amazed that none of the chairs had collapsed from the massive size of the bikers. Their height ranged from 6′3″ to 6′5″ and their weight from 230 to 300 pounds, all solid muscle. Ivan spotted Sally and Darlene in the pandemonium.

The lieutenant said, "We regret that one of the honorees was not able to be here today but he certainly will not be forgotten and will be honored at a later time."

Mr. Robins had spoken to the lieutenant earlier and asked him not to mention his name at the ceremony. He thought it would be best if he were to remain anonymous. In appreciation for his contribution, Ivan and the lieutenant would present Mr. Robins with a special plaque after the ceremony at his apartment.

The mayor stood and said, "Thank you all for coming today and for your support. This concludes our presentation."

The second event was for the police department to recognize its own. It was held the next evening in the banquet room at Melvin's restaurant. The station had reserved the back dining room at Melvin's for their special events dinner and celebration. Husbands and wives were invited and of course the star himself, Eduardo. Eduardo was unrecognizable as the under-cover guy. He was dressed to the hilt, immaculately groomed, quite handsome and he had even cut his pony tail. Melvin's had an outstanding buffet dinner set up consisting of everything imaginable and the champagne was flowing, but not too freely since it was a police event. Kudos were given to all of the lieutenant's team with special recognition for Ramon and Ted and Eduardo, the star himself, of course. After the ceremony, the crowd broke up and the close friends got together to go have a drink and to catch up with each other's lives since they had all been so busy. Everyone kept asking Sandy,

"Where did you learn to sing like that?"

Ramon said, "I didn't even know she could sing until I heard her in the shower one day! I thought it was the TV!!"

CHAPTER 49

Stephen could hardly wait to get home, relax with Donna and go out to dinner. When they got to Dominic's, they sat in a nice booth and ordered their drinks. It felt good to forget about work and enjoy talking to his wife. Something caught Donna's eye. She looked across the room and low and behold who did she see but her dad, Don, and his bridge partner, Connie. Donna told Stephen, and Stephen called the waiter over and asked him what the couple across the room was drinking. Their waiter said they had a drink before dinner and were going to select a bottle of red wine to go with dinner. Stephen chose a favorite red wine of his and Donna's and asked the waiter to send it over to them with their compliments. The waiter did so, and Don turned to where Stephen and Donna were sitting. Donna could see him smile and blush a little and they gave little waves to each other.

Donna said, "You know Stephen, San Pedro is a little town. You really can't get away with anything here. I'm glad dad is enjoying himself and going out more. Connie seems very nice. The next time we have a dinner I'm going to insist he bring her."

When they got home, Stephen said, "Honey, I hope you don't mind, but I am exhausted. I'm going to turn in early."

"I understand completely, Stephen."

"It's a good tired though, we accomplished a lot the past few weeks. I hope these criminals take a break for a change."

Donna laughed.

"I've got some things to do down here. I'll be up shortly."

CHAPTER 50

Stephen was awake when Donna came upstairs and joined him in bed.

"You know Stephen, I could use a trip to Catalina. How about you?"

"I thought you never took anyone with you?"

"That's true, I never have, but this time is special."

"How come?"

"Well, I thought maybe we could get married over there."

Stephen leaped straight out of bed.

"Do you mean it?"

"Yes silly, I thought we could surprise everyone later on without all the hoopla."

"Hallelujah!" Stephen cried out. Stephen gave her a big kiss.

"I love you, I love you, I love you," he said.

"Be ready to go first thing in the morning, Stephen. Call Ramon and tell him you have some personal